WAYNE GROVER

ALI and the GOLDEN EAGLE

Greenwillow Books, New York

Library of Congress Cataloging-in-Publication Data
Grover, Wayne.
Ali and the golden eagle / by Wayne Grover.
p.   cm.
Summary: An American working in Saudi
Arabia befriends a boy from a remote village
and helps him train an eagle to hunt.
ISBN 0-688-11385-0
[1. Saudi Arabia—Fiction.
2. Eagles—Fiction.]
I. Title.
PZ7.G93115Al   1993
[Fic]—dc20
91-43736   CIP   AC

This book is dedicated to Barbara, my wife and editor, who stayed home with the children while I traveled the world in search of adventure, and left me free to find Ali and the golden eagle.

Preface

SAUDI ARABIA is a country almost lost in time. With the exception of a few cities such as Jidda and Riyadh, most Arabs live in the traditions of their forefathers, who wandered the trackless deserts, raising sheep, camels, and goats.

Ali and the Golden Eagle is a story based on my experience from 1977 to 1979, while I lived in the remote highlands of western Saudi Arabia, near the great escarpment where the high plains of western Arabia drop rapidly off to the Red Sea some thirty miles away.

The Arabian Peninsula is tipped, being near sea level on the eastern Persian Gulf side and high and mountainous on the western Red Sea side. The high western region is one of the most remote places on the face of the earth: cold, barren, and nearly devoid of life-sustaining rain. I lived and worked in the most remote part of that region, just to the north of the Yemen border near the city of Khamis Mushayt, where the earth falls away into great canyons.

I worked for an American aircraft company that was building a modern airport and flight facilities in the midst of what had been a desolate plain just two years before. My job brought me in contact with several of the Saudi royal family, some of whom became close friends.

The culture of Saudi Arabia was and is restrictive. Photography was prohibited, along with a great number of other things Americans took for granted. I was once arrested for photographing baby goats in a public marketplace, jailed, and threatened with death. Many crimes carried the death penalty or were punished by chopping off limbs in public. Rape, theft, and any use of alcohol or drugs could result in beheading. When a Saudi royal princess fell in love with a non-Saudi, she and her lover were executed publicly in Jidda.

It was into this strange world that I and hundreds of other Westerners went on contracts with the Saudi government. I lived in a walled compound on the edge of the great canyon, and since I was a lifelong mountain climber, I explored the remote chasms at every opportunity.

It was during one of my explorations that I first saw the village called Ezratu. On my climb down to the village the first person I met was a shepherd boy named Ali. He, like most of the villagers of Ezratu, had never seen a Westerner before.

The people of Ezratu were self-contained, dependent on no outside source for anything. They had no modern appliances nor any power source, yet they had all the essentials for life. Although they lacked professional medical care, and several villagers were handicapped by limbs that had been twisted by accident and disease, their general state of health was robust.

Over a two-year period I made many climbs down to Ezratu. Once, after witnessing a falcon hunt, I asked if the villagers had ever trained an eagle to hunt. I was told that capturing an eagle was beyond their means because the birds lived high on the sheer, vertical rock walls of the canyon.

As an experienced climber with the right equipment I knew I might be able to reach a nest, and I soon located one high on the canyon wall. I succeeded in capturing an eagle chick and gave it to Ali's father. The gift resulted in my being accepted by the villagers. They gave me their friendship and trust.

When Ali and his golden eagle won a falconry contest, the village attracted attention, and many things began to change. I had mixed feelings about what I had started.

On my last visit to the village, in October 1979, electrical power was being installed by the Arabian government, and a road was being cut from the Red Sea coast. I knew things would never be the same. The villagers would have medical help and electrical power for lights and tools, but they would also face a much more complex life-style as they were exposed to the modern world.

Today the basic laws of Saudi Arabia have changed little. The status of women is still centuries behind what it is in Western countries. Saudi women are not even allowed to drive cars. When several brave Saudi women drove vehicles during a one-day demonstration early in 1991, their action was looked upon as against the law of the Koran, the Islamic holy book. They were strongly censured, and several holy men called for their execution.

During Operation Desert Storm in January and February 1991, the remoteness of Ezratu and its distance from the Persian Gulf and Iraq most likely created a buffer that shielded it from the massive influences of Western culture.

When I last heard about the real-life Ali, he was living in the city of Abha, where he had been educated. He was working for the Saudi Department of Conservation and Natural Resources and had taken a single wife, not four wives, as is the tradition of his country.

Although a great deal of this book is based on my personal experiences with Ali and his villagers, in writing this novel, I have dramatized some of the events and combined others to achieve a cohesive story, and some of the actual names of the people and places involved have been changed.

—*Wayne Grover*

Contents

1

The Great
Canyon

BOUNCING AND BUMPING along the rocky desert, leaving a trail of billowing brown dust, I saw a band of wild baboons scattering as I approached. The noisy Land Rover I was driving had startled them while they frolicked on the sloping plateau. They moved away in several directions, chattering excitedly.

A large male guarding the females and babies screamed and waved his long arms angrily when he saw my vehicle coming toward his group.

Just as I crested the next small rise, I had to jam on the brakes because several baboons were gathered right in front of me. The thick dust that was trailing the vehicle caught up and billowed past, surrounding me like a dark cloud.

When it cleared, I was surprised to see the big male sitting on the Rover's hood, peering in at me through the dust-covered windshield. Only the glass separated me from his ugly yellow teeth as he snarled fiercely, his lips pulled back.

He jumped up and down on the hood, shaking the vehicle from side to side, screaming and pounding threateningly on his massive chest.

Bam! Bam! With quick motions and brute strength, he hit the windshield with his hand-like front feet.

Bam! Bam!

The windshield broke, sending a web of cracks in every direction.

Bam! Bam! Bam! He kept hitting it, but the safety glass kept him from coming right in with me.

Jamming the Rover into gear again, I popped the clutch, and the vehicle jumped, dislodging the baboon, which agilely leaped aside. He ran after me for a few dozen feet but soon tired and stopped. Looking back over my shoulder, I saw the big male rejoin his band, still excited about my surprise visit.

I knew from past experiences that the wild baboons of the Arabian high desert could be very dangerous. The bands, numbering in the hundreds, hung around the walled-in living areas called compounds where foreign workers like me lived while in Arabia. The baboons were sometimes able to get inside the high protective wall and scavenge food from the refuse. To tangle with a full-grown male baboon would be asking for trouble, but as long as I stayed in my vehicle, I would be safe.

The morning sky was deep azure blue from horizon to horizon with not a wisp of a cloud in sight as I drove the Land Rover over the rocky terrain of the high Saudi Arabian desert.

When I first arrived in Arabia to fulfill a two-year contract to teach Saudi Arabians how to manage airports and radar systems, I expected the climate to be very hot and dry, and I wasn't disappointed. The Saudi Arabian capital of Riyadh sweltered in 120-degree ovenlike days.

I was pleasantly surprised to learn I would be assigned to the western side of Arabia, where the mountainous terrain created a cool climate all year. The city of Khamis Mushayt, where I lived while working for an American aircraft company, was at an elevation of nearly nine thousand feet, making the nights chilly and the days perfect.

My new boss told me there were a series of canyons close by, much like the Grand Canyon in Arizona, and I wanted to see them for myself. The first chance I got, I went to look for the canyons. It was exciting to be exploring the Saudi desert.

As I looked out across the high plateau, I saw nothing but rocky soil and scattered thornbushes. A few wild burros and camels were grazing on the sparse vegetation.

On the horizon rose a massive rocky mound that stood a good fifteen hundred feet above the flat plateau region, and I steered my Rover toward it.

I kept wondering how such a huge canyon could be hidden from my sight, but try as I might, all I could see was the rocky mound ahead.

I was driving about thirty miles an hour when suddenly, right in front of me, I saw the earth end! My heart leaped as I jammed on the brakes. The Rover skidded to a halt with the front wheels exposed over a canyon that dropped away for thousands of feet.

Very gently I shifted into reverse and backed into the swirling cloud of dust, away from the yawning chasm that had appeared from out of nowhere.

"Whew," I said aloud while I sat listening to my heart pound. Then I got out and carefully walked back to the canyon edge.

The sight that greeted me was so indescribably beautiful I was awestruck. I had been on a gentle upslope on the plateau which ran right up to the sharp drop-off. If I had looked away or had been driving faster, I would have hurtled out into space over a seven-thousand-foot drop.

After I had regained my composure, I reminded myself that Arabia was not Arizona. There were no roads to the canyon, no signs, and no safety rails. What I saw few Americans had ever seen. The great Arabian canyon dropped away in a dozen huge abysses that stretched as far as the eye could see. I was transfixed by its beauty.

Carefully I crept over to the edge and stood on a granite outcrop so I could look down into the canyon. The morning sun had not yet lighted the lower depths, making it appear dark and ominous, so far below me.

I had visited the Grand Canyon in Arizona, and it was indeed a spectacular sight, but the vast beauty of this remote chasm in far western Arabia took my breath away. I had never seen such sheer drops and vertically flat rock surfaces. It was as if a giant had cut the earth with an ax.

As I stood there with the cool morning wind blowing against me, I became aware of a soft, fluttering sound like a sail in the wind. The sound became louder and louder. Suddenly I saw them. Three large golden eagles were rising from deep within the canyon, using the warm air thermals to float upward. The fluttering was the air moving across their wing-tip and tail feathers.

The family of eagles soared up and out of the canyon almost at my feet and seemed surprised to see me there on the rim. They were evidently out for their morning hunt with the large male leading the way. I was struck by their size and beauty.

As they disappeared in the distance, other eagles rose from the canyon. Then hawks, falcons, and numerous smaller birds came up, too. I watched an unending parade of feathered creatures soaring up on the warm air. This remote part of the world was nearly untouched by modern people and their machines so the animal and bird life was in a natural state.

I walked along the edge with my binoculars hanging on my chest, watching the soaring birds, unaware of anything else.

Suddenly a movement caught the corner of my eye. A tawny-colored blur had raced out from a rocky outcropping and stood watching me. It was an old, scrawny lion as surprised to see me as I was to see him.

We stood there looking at each other while I wondered how many steps I could take back toward the Rover before he caught up with me.

The old lion didn't seem too anxious to bother me, and I certainly was not going to bother him. He watched me for a moment, then sat down as if he were tired and started scratching. Scratch . . . scratch. He yawned and lay down.

I had been told there were a few African lions left on this side of the Red Sea across from East Africa, but I never expected to see any.

I slowly backed up to my Rover, got in quickly, and closed the door. I needed some distance from the lion, so I started the engine and drove cautiously over the rock-strewn surface for about a mile.

I stopped, got out, and again stood on the canyon edge, studying the patterns and colors inside the great chasm. About two-thirds of the way down the near wall, I could see a sloping area that looked nearly level where the canyon wall gave way to a deeply gutted runoff. Water had scoured the earth for a million years to form ragged gullies.

Something about the flat brown surface looked a little different, so I put my binoculars to my eyes for a better view. I couldn't believe what I saw. There were houses on the flattened spot deep within the canyon.

I focused the glasses even tighter and could see people moving about. When I looked with my unaided eyes, all I could see was an uneven brown blur.

I walked along the rim until I was directly above the group of houses. Through the binoculars they appeared to be made from adobe like American Indian pueblos in Arizona and New Mexico. They had flat roofs, and some had raised towerlike structures, square in shape.

I decided to lie down on the ground and look into the chasm with just part of my head extending over the edge. The sun was just lighting the depths of the canyon with its scarlet morning glow, creating an array of subtle colors.

As I lay peering down at the strange sight, the faint sound of voices, carried by the wind, drifted up to my ears. I recognized the Islamic prayer call as the last word echoed from the canyon walls: "Allah . . . Allah . . . Allah . . . Allah . . ." It was the standard chant used by Muslims the world over when they assembled to pray.

I looked through my binoculars and saw several men and boys standing in three lines abreast while one man stood before them to lead the prayer. I aimed the binoculars around the village and saw the women assembled in their black chadors, praying separately in another area.

As I watched them say their prayers far below, I felt I had intruded on their private lives, so I pulled back and stood up. I wondered how the people of this remote village got out of the canyon. It was a mystery.

I thought about it for the rest of the day as I crawled over rocks and ridges, exploring the area near the rim of the canyon. I watched wild camels and burros grazing on tiny green leaves tucked deep in between long thorns on bushes and trees scattered across the desert.

As I headed back to the compound late that afternoon, I was still curious about the village deep in the canyon. I wanted to find a way to see it up close and perhaps meet some of the villagers in person.

Determined to accomplish that goal, I spent my free time after work the next week planning and gathering the supplies I would need.

2

New Friends

IT HAD BEEN a week since I discovered the canyon and the village nearly five thousand feet below the rim. I had two days off, my Rover was packed with food and water, and I had a new windshield.

Dawn was just breaking as I drove over the dusty, rock-strewn desert, and this time I knew where I was going and I was prepared.

Once I reached the rim of the canyon, I drove to the spot I had discovered the week before. There was a deep crevice in the canyon wall that started at the rim, splitting the rock wall, straight down, and ending above the village. It seemed to lead all the way down to the canyon floor near the village.

I had brought several hundred feet of nylon climbing rope and rappel equipment to help me drop into the canyon. In my backpack I also had full rock-climbing gear.

After blocking the Rover's wheels, I fastened the rope to the front bumper, threw the rope over the canyon wall, and watched as it dropped straight down.

I had never rappelled so far before. Going down would be easy because gravity would do all the work, but coming back up would be tricky and tiring. It would require using the rope brake, and I would have to set hand- and toeholds on the rocky face so that I could climb back up. I looked carefully at the chasm beneath my feet, for possible landing places on the rocks below.

After connecting the rope through the metal loops on my body harness, I took one last look at the Rover, checked that the hand brake was properly set and the wheel blocks were securely in place, then went over the side.

I dropped straight down for about thirty feet before my boots hit the rocky wall when I tightened the grip on my hand brakes. Loosening the grip, I shoved off and dropped another thirty feet. Like a bouncing ball on a string, I dropped slowly into the canyon.

To descend the nearly vertical rock face safely, I had to pound steel pins called pitons into small cracks, where they were attached to snap links to hold climbing ropes. Since I carried only two three-hundred-foot rope segments, I had to rappel down, set new pins, pull my rope through the links, and let it drop to me each time I reached its end. This way I could work my way down in segments, until I reached a place I could manage without ropes.

It was easy with the right equipment and my years of climbing experience, but I was alone, and that was danger-ous. Two of my British climbing companions had been plan-ning to join me, but they had to cancel their plans when they were called in to work at the last minute.

About four thousand feet down, I reached an area I could descend without a rope and carefully worked my way down for another thousand feet to where I could walk almost nor-mally.

Before me stretched an oasis of green, separated by rocky

ledges where ancient terraces were cut into the sloping valley floor.

As I looked in wonder at the fertile gardens growing on the flattened terraces carved into the steep slopes, a small voice called out in Arabic: "Who are you?"

I turned and saw a boy dressed in a white robe, wearing a red-checkered head cover. He looked frightened.

"I am an American. I've come to visit your village," I said in my best Arabic.

It was the first time I had tried my freshly learned Arabic since I graduated from the language institute prior to my assignment, and I was able to converse with the boy quite well.

"American? What is American?" the boy asked, still not sure of the stranger in his valley.

"I come from a land far away. It is called America. I am in Arabia to work for an American company that builds and flies airplanes."

"Where did you come from?" he asked.

I pointed toward the rim of the canyon and said, "I came from up there. I live a few kilometers from this canyon."

Watching the puzzled look on the boy's face, I realized he had probably never been out of this valley and had no idea about the rest of the world.

"My name is Wayne Grover. What are you called?"

"My name is Ali Zambir, son of Mustafa."

"Well, Ali Zambir, it is nice to meet you," I said as I offered my hand.

He paused, still unsure, then stuck his hand out to shake mine.

"I would like to visit your village, Ali. Can you take me there?"

Still uncertain about my foreign face and American clothes, he thought about my request before replying. "Yes, I will bring you to my father. He is the village chief."

He led me a long way, descending rocky slopes as we passed beautiful green terraces heavily laden with vegetables, pumpkins, gourds, and date trees. Each terrace had water running to it from a groove cut into the rocks above, where natural springs ran from the rock.

"I have never seen a man like you before, and your clothes are so strange," said Ali as we made our way down a long slope to his village.

I saw odd-looking structures made from what looked like brown mud. Each had a high flat roof and a tower that stood well above the main house. I saw clothes drying in the sun on the flat roofs as women, dressed all in black, busied themselves with their day's work.

"You live in a nice village, Ali," I said.

"*Shukran,*" he replied, which means "Thank you" in Arabic.

As we entered the only street in the village, many people came out to look at me. Women hid behind doors and peeped out, but the men watched me openly.

When we arrived at a large house, built into the side of the cliff, Ali called out, "Father! Father!"

An older man came out, greeted the boy, then asked about me.

"This is Mr. Wayne Grover from Ah-may-lee-ka," he told his father. "He came down the mountain like a spider on a long web. I saw it myself."

The man looked at me and smiled. "Welcome to my home, Wayne Grover. My name is Mustafa bin Abdul. Will you please take tea with me?" He turned and spoke to a woman peering from the roof. "Hayra, bring us tea."

I guessed she must be his wife or one of his wives since Muslim men can legally have up to four wives.

My first day in the secluded village was filled with new sights, scents, and sounds as my hosts entertained me. Most of the male children came to look at me, followed closely by their curious fathers. The women and girls kept their distance.

After hours of questions about the world I lived in, I felt hopelessly unable to explain. How could I describe cities and skyscrapers, superhighways and supermarkets, TV and moon rockets to a group of men and boys who, with a few exceptions, had never left their remote village?

Mustafa told me he and three other men had been to Khamis Mushayt, a local city, built on the old spice trade route traveled by camel-borne wanderers. Even so, they had seen only a few modern things. Just five years earlier Arabia was still a remote, mysterious place with barely any of the things we Westerners take for granted. For the most part the villagers could hardly imagine such wonders.

They listened to me but laughed and rolled their eyes when I tried to explain some of the inventions of the modern world. They all had seen an occasional plane fly high overhead. But it was just accepted as part of the evil world from which they remained hidden.

After we had finished our tea, Ali's father, using the Arabic word for "mister," a sign of respect, said, "Mr. Wayne, it would be an honor if you would allow me to take you on a tour of our village and show you how our people live."

"Mr. Mustafa, I would like that very much," I answered.

Then it was my turn to marvel.

Their houses were hundreds of years old, built and rebuilt from mud bricks with straw to hold them together. The stones lining the street were worn down from centuries of being walked on. The villagers had burros, sheep, and goats, and all were healthy and well fed. Almost everything was made by hand from the natural resources found in their isolated valley.

Mustafa showed me the way his people grew their own food on the rocky soil. I was amazed at the size and richness of the produce.

They baked their own bread, ground from wheat they grew on the terraces. They had a sweet jamlike substance from crushed berries grown nearby and wild honey from bee-hives they kept.

Their needs were simple, and they met them well. They seemed to live in harmony with the earth's cycles, farming, preserving, and recycling what they used. I was deeply impressed as I ended my visit.

I knew I had a long climb back up to the rim to where I left the Land Rover, and I would have to hurry to make it to the top before dark.

"Mr. Wayne," Mustafa said, "I will show you a way to climb up the cliff without using your rope. It is dangerous, but for an experienced man like yourself, you can return to the top much faster by climbing than by pulling yourself up with your rope."

As we walked up a rocky slope toward the place I was to start my ascent, I saw three Arabian men with large birds sitting on their arms.

"Do you train falcons here?" I asked.

Mustafa smiled proudly. "Yes, Mr. Wayne. I myself have five of the best hunting birds. Do you know about falconry?"

"Not much," I answered truthfully, "but I would like to learn more about it."

"Mr. Wayne, please visit us again soon, and I will show you how our falcons perform. You will see what a real Arabian and his falcons can do."

"Thank you, Mr. Mustafa. I look forward to coming again soon."

He led me to the base of the huge split in the rock wall

and showed me where he and a few village men had created a way to reach the world above.

As we stood at the entrance to the upward climb, he said, "Only a few men and I from our village have ever climbed to the world above our valley. We tried to bring supplies back from Khamis Mushayt, but the dangerous climb down was not worth the risk for the few items we could safely carry, so our villagers still live the way our ancestors taught us to.

"Be very careful, Mr. Wayne. There are a few dangerous places in the cleft in the wall. About halfway up, you will have to squeeze into a narrow place in the rock that is just big enough to pass. Once past that point, you will find several places where we have built handholds. I bid you a safe climb, and return soon to our valley. You are welcome here."

"Thank you, Mr. Mustafa. At the week's end I will have two days free from my work. I would very much like to return then, with your permission, and see more of your valley."

"Oh, Father," begged Ali. "Please say yes! We can learn much about the world from Mr. Wayne."

"Of course, my son. I also look forward to learning more about the outside world. You can meet Mr. Wayne when he returns and bring him to me."

Mustafa had assigned Ali, his youngest son, to look after me in the village because the older sons worked with him in the fields.

I noticed Ali's brother Faud frown when Mustafa asked Ali to meet me. Faud, the oldest boy, probably about eighteen or nineteen, was as large as I was and quite handsome. His brother Abdul, perhaps sixteen, was tall and thin.

Sensing a little jealousy, Mustafa explained, "I would ask my firstborn son to meet you and look after you, but he is a man and very strong; I need him and Abdul to work beside me. Faud will become village chief when I retire."

"I understand, Mr. Mustafa," I said, noticing Faud stand a little taller, basking in his father's praise.

"Well, then," I said, "Ali, I will return when the sun rises, six days from now."

"I will be here, Mr. Wayne. May Allah be with you until we meet again."

I entered the narrow chamber of rocky walls and soon was enjoying the challenge of finding the way back to the top. Within thirty minutes I found the narrow split in the rock that was about seventy-five feet from bottom to top.

It looked very narrow as I tried to squeeze my body into it and climb higher. It was like being cramped into a chimney, and for a moment I felt very uneasy. I thought about turning back, but I knew it was too late to get back down before dark, so I forced my body upward.

Both my chest and back dragged against the hard, rocky wall as I struggled to push upward. I had to breathe shallowly because when my lungs filled with air, I stuck where I was.

My heart was pounding and my lungs burned from the effort as I used my last strength to get out of the narrow passage. I knew it was no problem for a smaller man, but for someone my size, it was very confining.

The rest of the climb was easier. When I pulled myself onto the flat rim and stood up, darkness had already hidden Ali's village from sight, but I could see firelights flickering in the blackness. It had been a day of adventure and excitement, and I looked forward to seeing Ali, Mustafa, and the villagers again.

After walking to my Rover nearby, I drove across the desert toward my house in the compound. What had started as a mountain-climbing trip into the canyon had brought me new friends. I could hardly wait to visit them again.

3

Ali's First Climb

Six days later I was finally on my way back to the canyon. It seemed a shame to experience such beauty by myself, but the climbers among the British and Americans I worked with either had different shift schedules or were not inclined to tackle such sheer cliffs.

The sun had been up for half an hour as I headed out in the Land Rover. The surrounding mountains had a fiery fringe with the sun still behind them, and the desert itself was a light shade of pink from the dawn. It was a great day to be alive.

As I approached the canyon, I saw something in the distance. It was just a shape near the area of the rim where the passage began, but it was something I didn't remember being there before. When I finally got close enough to see what it was, I was surprised to see my new friend Ali, jumping up and down, waving his arms. He had apparently made the climb by himself.

As I pulled to a stop, he looked at my Land Rover with his eyes wide. He had never seen a motor vehicle before. I got out and stood there while he slowly got over his amazement at the dusty vehicle.

"Ali, how did you get up from the canyon floor?" I asked in surprise.

"I could not wait, Mr. Wayne. I decided to practice climbing up so I could meet you. Before I knew it, I was at the top. It was very exciting to climb, but I did not worry because I asked Allah to protect me. I have never been up here before."

"That was a very brave thing to do, Ali, but promise me you will not climb alone again. I want to be with you next time."

I was quickly learning that Ali was a very unusual and brave young man.

He took a deep breath and threw out his chest to its fullest. "I am very strong, Mr. Wayne. But I will not climb again unless you are with me. . . . What is that large machine you rode, Mr. Wayne?"

"This is called a jeep. It can carry four men and much weight, much more than any burro. Come, touch it. It won't bite you."

Ali's eyes were wide with awe as he carefully stepped up to the Rover. He reached out to touch it.

"My father told me and my brothers about this thing you call a jeep, but I could not imagine how it really looked. It is so large and strange-looking. I fear it," he said, looking to me for security.

"It is like the burros you ride in the valley, except it does not eat grass. It eats what we call gasoline," I explained. I unscrewed the cap of the spare gas can and stuck my fingers inside. "This is gasoline," I said.

Ali stuck his fingers in the can and pulled them out wet.

He stuck one finger in his mouth and suddenly spit out violently. "Mr. Wayne, this tastes terrible. How can your big burro eat it?"

I laughed out loud and wiped Ali's hand on my shirt. I knew that everything I took for granted would seem like a miracle to Ali, who had never in his life seen a machine, except an occasional aircraft high overhead.

"Ali, come, I will show you how my jeep 'eats' gasoline. Get inside."

He rolled his eyes and, unsure if he wanted to get closer, looked at the Rover. I opened the door and got in, patting the passenger seat with my hand. "Get in. I'll take you for a ride."

Ali carefully climbed into the seat and sat down. He looked at the dashboard with its instruments and then down to the floor, where there were two gearshift levers. His eyes were wide as he looked at things he never knew existed. He cautiously reached out and tried to pull the main gearshift out of the floor as he would a carrot from the ground.

He ran his hands over the dashboard and steering wheel. He turned the wheel a little, then sat back in utter amazement.

"Mr. Wayne, this is a strange burro."

"Jeep, Ali. Jeep," I said.

"Jeep," he repeated.

I pushed the horn button, and he jumped. I pushed it again. "See, my jeep calls out like your burros."

He reached and pushed the horn and drew his hand back quickly as it blew. He pressed it again and again, laughing loudly at the honking noise.

I started the engine and said to him, "Now we will take this big burro for a ride."

The Rover began to move, and Ali's eyes again opened

wide. I accelerated to about thirty miles an hour across the rocky plateau.

"Allah be with us!" he shouted above the engine's whine. We sped across a smooth, grassy area toward a rocky pond, where three wild burros were drinking. As I drove nearer, the burros jumped and ran away, while Ali watched with glee.

"There are many wild burros up here, Ali. Many of the Arabians now drive trucks and jeeps like this one, and their burros run free. It is the same with camels."

Ali sat entranced. I pointed out the sights as we bumped along, explaining each one as best I could.

"The world is so big, Mr. Wayne," he said in amazement.

"There is much more for you to see, Ali . . . much more," I assured him. "Come, Ali, I want to show you another 'miracle.'"

We got out of the Rover and walked to the canyon, where we could see for about sixty miles as it swept westward toward the Red Sea. I raised my binoculars and focused them for clear vision. I looked down toward the village below and saw the people and animals starting a new day.

"Here, Ali, look at your village." I held the glasses to his eyes and pointed them toward the village in the canyon.

Ali jumped back and said, "The rocks were flying to hit me."

I laughed. "No, Ali. These glasses allow you to see things that are far away and make them seem nearer."

He looked again and laughed out loud. "I can see my father's house, and there is Alazar the blacksmith by his shop."

He laughed in delight as he gazed down at his village far below.

"Mr. Wayne, I have very much to tell my father of the world up here. He will not believe what I have seen."

"Your father is a wise man, Ali. He knows about the

world and is wise enough to live his life in the peace of your village. You are lucky to have such a father."

I started to mention his mother, too, but I knew from experience that outsiders did not refer to Arabian women in conversation with their men.

As we stood on the canyon rim, a gentle, dry wind started to blow up from the great sweeping chasm, rustling Ali's white cotton tobe. We stood in silence, looking across the distance.

Then, from above, something caught my eye. Swooping down from high above the great canyon, a female golden eagle dived like a bullet. She tucked in her wings and gathered speed, hurtling faster and faster until she was nearly a blur.

Far below her a hawk, unaware of the danger speeding toward it, floated serenely on the warm updrafts rising from the sun-heated canyon. The hawk appeared well fed and lazy.

Like a lightning bolt, the eagle struck, talons first, grabbing the unwary prey in mid-flight. A flurry of feathers scattered as the eagle pumped her big wings to climb higher with her catch. The hawk struggled and fought to free itself, but it was no use.

The big eagle reeled in flight and flew straight toward a sheer wall of the canyon. She was joined by an even larger eagle, her mate, and together they flew, wingtip to wingtip, and seemed to disappear into the rocky face of the cliff.

From where we stood, we had a ringside seat while the great birds of prey hunted ground animals and sometimes each other. We watched the golden eagles with awe.

"I have never seen a more powerful bird than the golden eagles," said Ali. "They are so big and so fast in the air. If I could train one, I could be the best falconer in all the world."

One of the villagers had told me Ali's father was the best

falcon trainer in the great valley, and he had trained his sons to follow in his footsteps.

I thought about the eagles I saw flying straight into the cliff. I knew they hadn't just disappeared. From years of watching eagles in America, I knew they must have a nest with their young waiting for them to bring fresh meat to eat.

"Ali, why don't you train an eagle instead of a falcon?" I suggested.

"Oh, no, Mr. Wayne, no one has ever trained an eagle to hunt for them. The eagles live high in the canyon walls, where no man can ever reach them. My father has often said he wished he could catch a young one to train."

"Ali, I know a man who lived in Russia as a prisoner for twenty-seven years. He trained a huge black eagle to hunt for him outside the prison walls. He survived on the meat the eagle brought. He told me what a noble bird the eagle can be once it trusts a man. If he did it, you can, too."

"Just the thought of having such a great bird excites me," said Ali as we stood on the canyon wall and watched several other golden eagles soaring above the canyon, looking for prey.

Their wings, measuring more than six feet across, were gold-colored, tipped in white. As they glided on the warm thermal air currents, I could hear the wind rippling over their wingtips and tail feathers. The warm air gently passing over their feathers made a whirring, fluttering sound.

Eagles usually hunted in the morning hours, when the air was cool and heavy, then floated lazily in the late afternoons on the warm updrafts after they had eaten their fill.

Many other large birds abounded in this canyon on the far western edge of Arabia, directly across from the African continent. It was my guess that it contained one of the largest natural collections of predatory birds left in the world.

Ali and I spent most of the day exploring. We had an American picnic with sandwiches and fruit I had brought from the compound. Ali was amazed at the sliced bread and had never seen or tasted an apple before.

After we had eaten, we just stood watching the birds from the canyon rim. We saw eagles, hawks, falcons, vultures, and many varieties of other hunting birds. There were also dozens of species of smaller birds that flitted in and out of their nests along the canyon walls. Far below, on the canyon floor, lived foxes, baboons, antelope, rabbits, and many other furry creatures that managed to survive in the desolate region.

As the day grew late and the sun inched lower in the western sky, it was time to get Ali back to his village. His father would be worried about him.

"Mr. Wayne, would you like to return with me to my village and eat with my family?"

I knew I would have to spend the night in the village because it would be dark before I could climb back out, but I liked the idea.

"Yes, Ali. I would like to meet your family and the villagers again. Let's climb down together. I'll go first."

I knew the Rover would be okay left alone on the rim. One of the nicest things about Arabia was that there was virtually no crime. No one would touch the locked vehicle.

The climb down into the canyon took about an hour and was dangerous to anyone not knowing the exact route to take. Ali followed me like a mountain goat, surefooted and agile. He had the bottom of his long white tobe tucked into his underpants while we climbed.

Every few minutes he called down to me, "Mr. Wayne, can you make it?"

"I think so, Ali," I answered.

Finally we reached the bottom and stood on the steeply

sloped hills that led to his village. Darkness had come to the canyon as we made our way toward the firelights flickering from the houses.

The smell of spices and woodsmoke floated on the gentle breeze. I could hear sheep and goats bleating as we set foot on the rocky street. It was like a *National Geographic* television special, but I was living it instead of watching it.

The village women, true to Saudi tradition, never showed themselves to strangers. I seldom got more than a fleeting glimpse of them, dressed in long black gowns with black veils covering their heads and faces as they moved about.

For a thousand years the people of this isolated village had lived the same way. Their lives were simple and happy. They toiled, raising their food from the arid land they had terraced and watered with springs oozing from the canyon walls. They grew rich vegetables, pumpkins, and gourds, which they gathered and stored for the winter. They also raised animals: sheep to provide wool for clothing and goats to provide milk and cheese. But the best food of all was the small game their hunting falcons brought back, providing them a selection of tender meats to feast on.

Many Arabians, even the royal family, trained falcons, but the villagers knew more about them than anybody else since they used the birds every day to hunt for food.

"Mr. Wayne, my father said that the next time I bring you to the village, he would like to enter into a contest of strength with you. He wants to show the villagers that he is stronger than you. He is the strongest man in our village."

The Saudis respected muscle. Without strength, it would be difficult for them to survive the harsh conditions in which they lived. Since I was larger than most of the villagers, Mustafa thought this would be a good opportunity to prove his strength once again.

We passed several houses in the village before we came to Ali's. It had the tallest tower standing above the flat roof, marking it as the village chief's home.

"Father! Father! I am home, and I have Mr. Wayne with me," called Ali as we approached the stairs to the house.

"Enter, with Allah's blessing," invited his father.

I heard the rustling of the women's dresses as they disappeared from sight.

Together we climbed the stone stairs to the house.

4

A Test of Strength

"AH, WELCOME to our home, Mr. Wayne." Ali's father greeted me in traditional Arabian style. "May Allah bless you and your children."

Mustafa was larger than most Arabian men. His handsome face was set off by a black goatee and mustache.

"And may Allah give you health and many more children," I replied, greeting him politely as Arabians greet one another.

Mustafa's piercing dark eyes looked much like the falcons he trained, but a warmth and sincerity poured from them, making me feel welcome in his home and village. He added, "And may you prosper and live long."

With the customary greeting over, Ali's brothers came and shook my hand one by one. "My father says he wishes you to try your strength against his, Mr. Wayne," said Faud, the oldest of Mustafa's sons.

"Your father looks very strong, and I am sure I can be no match for him," I said, showing respect for the boy's father and hero. "Ali told me that he is the strongest man in the village and that he has been the contest champion for many years."

"That is true," replied Faud. "And he will beat you."

Ali and his brothers were justly proud of their father. They, in turn, were the light of his eye.

Mustafa told me he had three wives, one fewer than allowed by the Koran. He also had five daughters, but Saudi men never speak of their daughters with anyone outside the family. The Saudi families love their daughters just as much as their sons, but centuries-old tradition and religious practices require the women to remain separate when outsiders are in their homes.

"Come, my American friend, let us share food together."

Mustafa sat down on the hand-woven carpet that was spread on the earthen floor of the eating room and gestured for his sons and me to join him. As we ate together, I was careful to use only my right hand to touch the food. Arabians never use their left hand to eat, and I did not want to offend my host.

Mustafa, his four sons—Faud, Abdul, Ali, and Raman, Ali's full brother—and I sat in a small circle around the food, which was served in dishes placed on the floor mat. They enjoyed a tasty meal of goat meat, rice with cheese, and steaming vegetables.

After finishing our meal, we went out onto the flat roof of the house. It was a velvet black night, and the stars shone with brilliant intensity.

"Allah is watching over us. See his big cup pouring forth goodness on our village," Mustafa said, pointing to the Big Dipper. "It is a good omen."

We all sat for about an hour on the stone ledge of the roof in the blackness of the canyon night and talked. The only sound was the rustle of the wind as it stirred the trees in the groves near the houses.

"You can sleep in the tower, Mr. Wayne, and tomorrow we will have the contest of strength."

I wasn't sure what kind of contest I was in for, but I knew that if I was going to win the confidence of Ali's father and brothers, I had better make a good showing.

"Yes, I hope I can do well," I replied.

The tower of the old stone and mud house, hundreds of years old, had once been used as a lookout post when the warring tribes of the canyon raided each other's villages, but through the years it had come to be used for many other purposes. Now, in a time of peace, the tower, with its two interior levels, was used for food storage and the sheltering of animals when the winter winds blew through the canyon.

Mustafa prepared a bed of straw under a handwoven wool blanket and bade me good-night. I felt a sense of peace and beauty as I lay there. The smell of drying hay and pumpkins filled the air. Soon I was in a deep sleep.

"Wake up, my friend. Wake up." It was Ali, shaking my shoulder and smiling broadly as he greeted me in the new day.

"Good morning, Ali." I yawned.

"Good morning, my Ah-may-lee-can friend. We have finished our morning prayers, and it is time for you to rise."

I stretched and stood to look out the big open window. The day was bright and clear, and I could see for miles down the canyon. The rising sun lit the rim above the canyon like a halo of fire. Ali stood by my side. We watched several large birds repeatedly swooping toward the ground, hunting rodents that scurried along the canyon floor.

"It is a wonderful day to have a contest and hunt with the falcons, is it not?" asked Ali.

"Indeed, it is. I look forward to seeing your father work with his birds."

I followed Ali down to the main level of the house, where the women had set out breakfast. I joined the male family members on the meal mat, and my Arabian friends served me their traditional treat, fresh pumpkin with a spicy sauce mixed with rice and meat.

"When the sun is high and the work is finished, we will show you true Arabian hospitality, my friend," said Mustafa, wiping his mouth.

"I look forward to it, Mr. Mustafa."

"Please, just call me Mustafa. As friends we need not be so formal."

"I agree, and I would like you to call me Wayne."

After we had finished eating, Mustafa and his three older sons went to work their fields. He asked Ali to stay behind with me.

"Come, Mr. Wayne, I'll show you more of the village and the fields."

He led me down the stone street that sloped steeply toward the canyon floor, hundreds of feet below. As we walked, Ali pointed out the sights. "See, there is the baker's store. He makes bread for all the village. And there is the iron forger. He makes our tools for farming the land."

Everywhere I looked, the villagers were busy going about their daily lives. As we walked down the street, I noticed the women go into their houses and not reappear until after we had passed.

Ali and I walked through the canyon, watching the wild creatures in their search for food and survival. Finally we came upon a large band of baboons scattered along a sloping hill.

"Stop here," warned Ali. "The baboons can be very dangerous. See those big males away from the others. They are the guards and will attack anything that comes near their females and babies. We have lost two villagers to them in the past year."

As I looked at the big animals, they were already moving toward us. The lead baboon must have weighed as much as I did.

"Run, Mr. Wayne. He looks angry," warned Ali. We turned and hurried back up the canyon.

It was just after noon when we returned to the village. About thirty men and boys were assembled in a clearing of grass, waiting for the third prayer of the day. Ali hurried to join them.

When Mustafa called the prayer, all the men stood in rows facing toward the city of Mecca to the north. Mustafa stood alone in front of them. Then they assumed a kneeling position, and for five minutes they alternated positions by placing their foreheads on the ground, then returning to an upright kneeling position. Mustafa led the prayers with an Arabic songlike chant. They finished and stood up. "Now we shall compete in the contest of strength," called Mustafa. "Wayne, my American friend, do you think you are as strong as I?"

"Your sons have told me of your great strength, Mustafa. I can only hope my own strength is sufficient to warrant a contest," I answered.

"You will see that we are a very strong people," said Faud.

An old white-bearded man stepped forward. Ali explained to me that he was the judge.

"Who shall be first in the contest?" he asked.

Two village men stepped forward, faced each other, and grabbed each other's forearms near the elbows in a tight hand lock. The old man shouted the command to start the contest. Each man tried to force the other off his feet and throw him to the ground. They grunted and groaned and struggled until suddenly one man lost his footing and was sent flying.

The victor shouted, "As Allah wills it!"

Man after man tried his hand at beating the winner but soon ended up on the ground.

Finally Ali's father was the only man left who had not tried. He stepped into the contest circle and grabbed the big Arabian's forearms.

"Start!" called the judge.

The two strong men pushed and pulled, trying to throw the other off-balance. They both were skilled at the contest, and I could not help wondering what would happen to me when my turn came.

With a mighty heave, Mustafa nearly lifted his opponent from his feet and sent him flying to the ground. The villagers cheered while he raised both hands in victory.

"Mr. Wayne, you have seen that my father is the champion of the village. He has also beaten the best men of the other three villages in the valley. His father before him was also champion." Ali was looking up at me with a proud smile on his face.

"Yes, he is very strong, Ali. He is truly a great champion."

"If you try his strength, you will lose, too, Mr. Wayne. No one has ever beaten my father."

Just then the villagers started calling together, "Let the American try! Let the American try!"

Mustafa, sweating and smiling, looked at me and said,

"Yes, now let me show you Arabian strength, my American friend."

The time had come to try my luck against the champion. I took off my jacket and rolled up my shirtsleeves. I had no idea what I could do against such a strong man, but I would do my best.

I stepped into the circle and faced Mustafa squarely. We shook hands, and then I slid both my hands up his arms until they were locked around them at the elbow.

His hands, as tough as tanned leather, felt like a vise around my arms. We stood there, face-to-face, waiting for the signal from the starter. The command to begin was shouted by the judge.

Mustafa was so fast that I was almost thrown to the ground in the first second. He had exceptional strength, and I struggled to keep my balance.

The villagers cheered for their chief as I tried to stay within the circle formed by small stones. I would need some advantage if I were to have a chance. I tried to push him back, but he bent his knees and lowered his shoulders and stood like a rock. With all my might, I pushed and pulled, but he didn't budge. Then he gave a grunt and lurched forward with all his strength, nearly forcing me down. It gave me an idea.

When I took karate lessons, I had learned to use an opponent's strength against him, using balance and speed to alter his direction. Maybe it would work here.

I started pushing forward until I felt Mustafa shove back. He took a deep breath and attacked. As he pushed forward, I let my arms go loose, and he shot toward me, off-balance; his feet were not planted tightly, so I twisted as hard as I could.

In that instant Mustafa proved he was the stronger man.

Regaining his balance, he suddenly lifted me off my feet and easily threw me out of the contest circle. I hit the ground with a thump. A loud cry rang out from the villagers as I sprawled on the ground.

Slowly I stood up, and Mustafa looked at me with a deep frown. Then, suddenly, with a smile that seemed to spread from ear to ear, he threw his arms around me and enthusiastically thumped me on my back. "You are very strong, my friend, but not strong enough!"

"You have beaten me squarely, Mustafa. I salute you!"

The villagers laughed and cheered. I was suddenly no longer a stranger. I was one of them.

"Abdul, prepare the falcons. We shall show our American friend true Arabian mastery of the skies."

I knew I was in for a treat that few outsiders had ever shared. I was going to see the masters of falconry work with the fierce predators of the sky.

5

The Falcons

"COME, MY FRIEND. We will go to the falcon house, and I will show you the fastest, strongest birds ever to hunt for man. You will see we have the finest birds in the world."

Mustafa, followed by his sons and me, led the way to the long mud-brick building, covered with a heavy thatched roof.

As we entered, I was greeted with the pleasant smell of earth and leather. The building was clean and had air vents spaced along the walls, just under the roof.

There was a long row of perches along both sides of the main aisle down the middle of the building. Each perch had a large bird on it, attached to its roost by a leather strap. Each strap was short enough to keep the birds from reaching one another. I quickly learned why they were kept that way.

As Mustafa stopped and spoke with three teenage boys who were preparing some of the falcons for the hunt, I walked close to a large dark bird. In an instant the huge bird leaped from its perch and flapped its wings to jump on my left arm, digging its razor-sharp talons into my flesh. With its beak it slashed at my face and neck.

It happened so fast that I just stood there until Ali grabbed the leather thong and pulled the bird away. The bird let out an ear-piercing scream and beat its wings, trying to fly away.

"Mr. Wayne, these birds let only their own masters come close to them, and they can be very dangerous," said Ali. "They can rip your eyes out with their beaks. Please, stay behind my father until we select and blindfold our birds."

Faud was smiling at my discomfort, seeming to enjoy it.

My arm was bleeding from wounds where the falcon had tried to land, but I knew it was my fault, not the bird's. When their masters took them on their left arms, the arms were wrapped in heavy leather and the birds were hooded. The bird that had jumped on my arm was only doing what came naturally.

"Aha, Mr. Wayne, you have met Kitcha. She is one of our best hunters. She must like you or you would not have any eyes left," said Mustafa, laughing.

"Yes, I am fortunate to have met such a nice bird," I said, laughing back.

"Faud, go bring us some warm water and a clean cloth wrap so I can clean up Mr. Wayne's arm."

While we waited for Faud to return, Mustafa took me on a tour of the aviary. As I looked at the big birds, I could see there were true falcons among a larger collection of hawks. I knew that falcons differed from hawks by their long, sharp-pointed wings and longer tail feathers. Both have keen eyesight and ferocity, but the hawks tend to be a bit heavier and slower in flight.

Kitcha, a female peregrine falcon with piercing eyes and a pointed, turned-down beak, looked almost regal with her thick, shiny black feathers, tipped in brown and white.

"Kitcha is one of our best hunters, but she will let only my father and me near her," said Ali, picking up a woolen blanket. He threw it over the falcon's head, and she quieted immediately.

Next, he attached both her feet to the roost bar with short leather loops. He took a hood made from goat's leather and another leather thong about fifteen feet long and held them at the ready.

Lifting the blanket from the bird's head, he carefully slipped the hood over her. It had a place for her beak to protrude but covered her eyes so she could not see. He attached one end of the short strap holding her to a small wooden ring on his leather-covered left arm, then placed the arm against the bird's chest, and she stepped onto it, fluttering her wings as she found her balance.

"There, you see? She is ready for the day's hunt."

Faud returned with a wooden bowl nearly full of hot water steaming in the cool air. It smelled like camphor as Mustafa washed the scratches on my arms and face.

"There, you are as good as new," he said as he wrapped a soft handwoven cloth around my arm.

Ali looked small with such a big bird on his arm, but he was all smiles as we started out with the six men Mustafa had chosen to work their birds that day.

Each man had a bird on his arm as Mustafa led the procession with another of his own birds, a brownish female falcon, regally perched on his arm, still as a statue.

"My father's falcon is the fastest hunter in the world," boasted Ali. "She will get more game than any of the others. You'll see."

We walked a long way from the village until we were on a ridge that dropped off steeply on each side. I could see dry riverbeds where the water from centuries of runoff had scoured the canyon bottom on its rush to lower ground and eventually to the Red Sea.

The hunters stopped and separated, each man with his falcon on his left arm, hooded and quiet. Ali's bird was nervous and kept jumping up but was held in place by the leather strap attached to its feet.

"First, my father will work with his falcon and then let it start the hunt," Ali explained to me. "This is very important because man is the natural enemy of these birds, and we must let them know we will feed them. This is done by using a long leather strap with a goatskin-wrapped pouch on the end. The pouch has bird wings sewn onto it and a piece of raw meat tied to it. The bird is fed from the hand at first to let it know it will always get food from its master," continued Ali.

Mustafa, listening as his youngest son explained some basics of falconry to me, smiled proudly, and said, "Ali has a special way with birds, and at thirteen, he is probably a better falconer than most of the adults."

"But, Father," interrupted Faud, "am I not better than Ali?"

Mustafa lowered his eyes and paused. "Yes, Mr. Wayne, Faud is also an excellent falconer."

Faud's eyes showed his feelings of jealousy and resentment for his father's attention to young Ali. He stared hard at him and stalked away without speaking further.

Mustafa took the hood from his bird and fed it meat from a pouch tied to his waist. The big bird snatched the meat with its sharp beak and raised its head to swallow it in one piece. The bird watched intently as Mustafa tied two pieces of meat to the small pouch on the end of the long thong and swung the pouch in a big circle. He released the bird, and in an instant it caught the pouch and ripped the meat from it, swallowing it in mid-flight.

The procedure was done twice more, and each time the bird landed back on its master's arm.

"Now is when we must trust the bird to go back to its freedom, hunt for us, and return with the game it has captured. If the falconer has not gained the bird's trust, it will fly away to stay," explained Mustafa.

As we watched, Ali's father raised his arm high, then quickly dropped it. The falcon took flight. It flew around Mustafa several times, let out a shrill call, and flew down toward the valley below.

One by one, the other men went through the same routine until all six birds were gone off to hunt.

"Now, my son, it is time for both you and Kitcha to learn," said Mustafa.

"We are ready, Father."

Mustafa took a mask made from interwoven bamboo strips and slipped it over his son's head. He then wrapped a long piece of cloth around his son's neck.

"Now, son, slowly uncover the bird's head, but keep her tightly held to your arm. Easy now."

Ali very carefully reached over with his right hand and pulled the cover from the falcon's head. As he did, the big bird instantly slashed out at the mask on Ali's face.

Ali stood still as the bird tried to bite him. He seemed to have no fear.

"Very good, my son. Stand still, and do not be afraid. The bird will sense you have no fear and stop trying to hurt you."

Little Ali stood steady with the big bird flapping her wings and slashing at him. I wondered how such a young boy could be so brave.

"Now, feed the bird some meat, but be careful."

Ali reached into his meat pouch and took out a small piece of bloody meat. As he moved it toward the falcon, the bird snatched it with a lightning movement, catching Ali's fingers in her sharp beak. I saw blood ooze from his fingers, but he showed no trace of pain or fear. He reached in and again gave the bird another piece and again was bitten on the hand.

"Son, you must withdraw your hand as the beak grabs the meat. Try it again."

This time Ali managed to retract his hand without being bitten. The watching falconers gave a nod of approval.

"Well done, my son! One day you will be the greatest falconer in the world. Now I shall show Kitcha the meat. Then I will swing it in a circle, and you can let her fly after it on the long lead."

"As you say, Father."

Mustafa held the meat close to the falcon's mouth and teased the bird with it. When she tried to snatch it from his hand, he quickly pulled it back. He soon had the bird excited and struggling to be free of the restraints holding her.

"Release her, but hold the line tightly," Ali's father called out.

With a flurry of wings, the big bird flew from her perch on Ali's arm, reaching the end of her tether in a split second. Mustafa swung his meat lure around and around while the falcon struggled to get to it. The bird pulled so strongly that Ali had difficulty holding on to the tether.

Mustafa walked in closer so that the arc of his swinging meat pouch came near the falcon's tether limit. In an instant the bird grabbed the pouch from mid-flight and ripped at it with its beak.

"Aha! She has struck," called Ali.

"Yes, your bird is swift, my son, but it will take many lessons before she will learn to hunt for you alone. She still wants to fly to me. If you can become Kitcha's trusted master, she will hunt well for you."

Over and over Ali and his father repeated the training process, each time giving the bird a little more length of line so she could fly a bit higher above their heads.

"How long does it take to train a bird?" I asked Mustafa.

"Sometimes it takes a year or more to get a bird to hunt and return with its catch. It is natural for birds to eat what they catch so they must know they will receive good care from their master and be well fed. Some birds never learn. Kitcha is a fine hunter. She and Ali still need much training together."

After about forty minutes of standing on the hill watching Mustafa and Ali train Kitcha, the other men started watching the sky for the return of their falcons.

"It is Lota returning!" One of the falconers was shading his eyes from the sun and pointing to a bird flying up from the valley below.

"No, it is Basrok," shouted another.

As the bird approached, I saw it was carrying an animal in its talons. The bird swooped high overhead and then dived for the group of men on the ridgetop. It came in fast, dropped its catch at its master's feet, then folded its wings and landed on his arm.

"You see, it is my Basrok," said the proud falconer. "He has brought me a fine rabbit for the table." He took out a large piece of meat and gave it to the bird, which gobbled it down in one bite. Then he gave Basrok another piece.

One by one the birds returned with game. Some had animals; others had birds. Mustafa's falcon brought a small lamb. When the men saw it, they groaned as one.

"By the hair of a she goat, Lubika has stolen a lamb from one of the lower villages," complained Mustafa. "I shall have a visitor within two sunsets to claim our village falcons have raided their flock again."

I whispered to Ali, "Will this cause a big problem for your father?"

"No, Mr. Wayne. We shall have a feast with them, drink lots of coffee and tea, and give them one of our lambs. It happens many times. Their falcons raid our flocks, too."

It was late afternoon when we all returned to the village. The canyon was already in deep shadow, with just a patch of blue sky overhead. It was time for me to start back to the canyon rim. I knew the climb out would take until dark, so I thanked my guests for their hospitality and said good-bye.

"We look forward to your next visit, Wayne. If you will call down when you return to the rim, I will send Ali up to meet you," Mustafa told me. "Ali, you may walk with our American friend to the cliff face where he will begin his climb."

"Thank you, Father," a happy Ali replied.

I shook hands with Mustafa and his three other sons.

As Ali and I walked to the cliff, we saw three golden eagles lazily circling in the warm air thermals of the canyon's updrafts, high above.

An idea that had been going through my mind became clearer. I had already talked with Mustafa about it and received his permission to have Ali join me in exploring the area above the canyon again. He told me he wanted Ali to learn more about the "world" above the canyon village and was confident that as a good friend I would look out for his son's best interests and safety.

Watching the eagles, I said, "Ali, if we could capture an eagle, you and your father could train the mightiest bird in the world to hunt for you."

Ali looked at me curiously. "It is not possible to catch the eagles. They live in huge nests made from sticks high in the canyon walls. No man can reach them there."

"Maybe the time has come to find out," I said as I started up the first steps cut into the stones. "I have an idea. The next time I come to see you, I may have a surprise."

"Go with Allah, Mr. Wayne."

"May Allah protect you," I called back.

Darkness came quickly, and I just managed to reach the canyon rim as the last light faded into blackness. I got into my Rover and started toward the compound where I lived.

6

The Dangerous Cliff Face

I KNEW just what was needed. After years as a mountaineer I had climbed many peaks from the bottom up. Now, to locate a baby eagle, I had to climb down instead.

I knew that eagles lived in small caves and along ledges on the sheer face of canyon walls, hundreds of feet from the bottom or top. There they safely raise their young, away from all danger.

To get to an eagle's nest, I would have to locate one and then drop straight down from above and take the smallest one of the young while its parents were away hunting. I knew that the first-hatched eaglet usually killed its younger, weaker siblings, so I would be saving an eagle baby's life if I could capture it for Ali before it was too late.

Each evening after work I looked for the things I would need to get down the canyon wall. Basically I needed some angle iron, long metal spikes, and heavy-duty rock anchors, plus my regular climbing gear.

All my friends in the compound where I lived enjoyed hearing about Ali and his family as we dined together each evening in the large mess hall. Most were Americans like me, but many were from Britain. Some had brought with them various items to be used for personal hobbies, including mountain-climbing equipment. They all were willing to donate or exchange anything they had to help with my mission to get an eaglet for Mustafa.

By week's end I had everything I needed and two days off, so I drove out to the canyon wall. It was a bright morning in early May, the time of year the big birds hatched their young. I sat on the rim of the canyon and watched and waited for the eagles to appear as they hunted for food.

It wasn't long before I saw two golden eagles flying together, wingtips nearly touching. They were hunting as a team. The male eagle would fly down the valley and try to scare up an animal. If he missed, the female came swooping in from another direction, usually catching the unwary prey as it ran from her mate.

After watching several eagles and hawks hunting, I saw a golden eagle fly toward the canyon wall and seemingly disappear. I knew it must have a nest there.

I made mental note of the landscape above the area from which the eagle had disappeared and then drove there. I carefully approached the canyon rim and looked down. I waited for several minutes before I saw an eagle below me, carrying something in its talons.

It was a female golden eagle. She slowed down and disappeared from my view. She had landed on her nest, perhaps 150 feet to my right and about 500 feet down the rock wall.

I carefully worked my way until I was directly above the nest. I picked up several big stones to mark the spot so I could find it again. Now I knew where the eagles lived.

I drove to the area of the rim above Ali's village and got out. I cupped my hands and shouted, "Aliii . . . ! Aliii . . . !" My voice echoed across the canyon, and I could hear

"Aliii . . . Aliii . . . Aliii . . ." as each echo became weaker and finally faded out.

Looking through my binoculars, I saw several villagers working in the terraced fields. Some stopped and looked around to see where the voice was coming from.

Again I shouted, "Aliii . . . ! Aliii . . . !"

After the echo had disappeared, I heard Ali calling back with his centuries-old Arabian greeting. It sounded like the warble of a bird, a high-pitched sound made by moving the tongue rapidly against the roof of the mouth.

"Can . . . you . . . come . . . up?" I called, spacing each word for clarity.

Again the echoes resounded, and when they were finished, I faintly heard his reply. "Yes . . . I . . . will . . . come!"

Within an hour Ali's head poked over the rim. "Allah be with you," he called.

"And with you." I replied. "Ali, I have a surprise for you. Today we will build a way to catch an eagle baby. I have everything we need in my Rover. Come, we have much work to do."

As we unloaded the rope and other items, Ali asked what each was. His inquisitive mind was like a sponge. I carefully explained what we were going to build, and I could see his excitement.

The plan was simple. We would anchor spikes into the canyon rim, then attach a frame to hold a spindle of rope. The rope would be let down the cliff face, and I would rappel down to the nest area. Getting down to the nest would be one thing, but getting back up with an eaglet in a bag would be another.

If I went down while the parent eagles were there, they would surely attack me. My descent would have to be timed just right.

We set to work, preparing the device and checking how long the eagles stayed away while hunting. On the average, they were gone about thirty minutes, sometimes longer, sometimes less.

By midmorning we had everything ready. The frame was made of metal, bolted together, and staked into the earth by long spikes. Within the frame was a thick metal roller with the long rope attached to it. That way the climber could either work up the rope if it was locked in place or be assisted up by a toothed gear lock winch, wound up by the person on the top.

I explained to Ali how we would proceed. "The eagle's nest is directly below us. I will go down to see if there are eaglets in it. We will have to work together, and you will hold my life in your hands once I drop over the edge."

Ali looked troubled. "Mr. Wayne, I am afraid. I do not know how to use this thing you call a winch."

"Ali, we will practice until you know exactly how to work this winch. It is safe if you do exactly as I tell you. Now watch me while I show you how it works."

I pulled out a long length of rope and placed it over the pulley staked securely to the rim, right at the vertical drop. The main winch built into the steel frame was back from the cliff wall about three feet. The pulley would let the rope glide smoothly without being cut by the friction and weight it would hold later. It dropped into empty space and then stopped as it caught tightly on the roll-up spindle.

"Now, Ali, this is how you will help get me back up once I descend down the rope to the eagle's nest."

I cranked the winch slowly in a clockwise motion, and the steel gearbox clicked loudly as each tooth grabbed hold against the lock mechanism. Clickity clack, clickity clack. The rope moved smoothly up from the canyon and was quickly rewound.

"It is a miracle, Mr. Wayne. I have never seen such a thing as this. I could let myself down to the village on such a—how do you call it, 'machine'?"

"Winch," I said, "a winding machine."

I attached a bag full of rocks to the steel-reinforced loop at the rope's end and reversed the winch lock. Clickity clack, clickity clack, the bag slowly dropped down into the canyon pulled by its own weight.

I had rigged up a secondary emergency brake, a long steel rod that could be shoved into the gear mechanism. If anything happened, the rod could be shoved in to lock it, but I would have to climb up using hand brakes on the ropes, a very tiring and slow process.

I would be carrying four of the small steel brakes in my jacket pocket when I went over the side. If something happened to the winch, or if Ali made a mistake, I could fall about five hundred feet straight down but would be stopped when the rope reached its end, where it was securely attached to the winch. I hoped my emergency backups would not be needed, but after twenty years of mountaineering, I knew to expect the worst and prepare for it.

The bag of rocks slowly went down, and I stopped its descent about two hundred feet down the canyon wall.

"Ali, pretend that bag is me down there. I will call three commands to you once I go over the side. They are 'down,' 'stop,' and 'up.' If I call, 'Down!,' you pull this lever toward you and crank the winch this way." I slowly cranked the winch counterclockwise, and the bag went down farther.

"If I say, 'Up!,' push the lever this way and crank like this." I then showed him how to reverse the gear lock lever and crank clockwise.

"If I say, 'Stop!,' just stop cranking, and the winch lock will hold me where I am. Do you understand?"

How quickly he caught on. When I let him take the handle and said, "Up," Ali immediately pushed the gear lock to the correct position and started cranking the bag up the cliff face. When I said, "Down," he reversed the lever and let the bag down until I said stop.

"Ali, you did it exactly right."

"Mr. Wayne, this machine fascinates me. I have a funny feeling when I see it work. I felt the same thing when you showed me your Rover machine. I cannot explain it, but it makes me feel light and tingly inside."

I wondered if I had started something that might change Ali's life by showing him things that most of his fellow villagers had never seen before. They were strong, healthy, and happy people without a TV to watch or cars to drive. I knew Western culture would come to the village soon enough, and it troubled me to think about what it might do.

I put Ali through the paces of letting the bag of rocks down and then winding it up. I would call: "Up! Down! Up! Down! Stop!" His strong, deft hands obeyed.

He never got tired of winding, and his ever-present smile seemed to brighten as he put his muscle power into the action of bringing the bag back up.

When we stopped to eat lunch, Ali was in store for a few new surprises. I had packed an insulated cooler with ice cubes, food, and cold drinks from the big refrigerator in the dining hall where I had eaten an early breakfast.

Remembering our first picnic, Ali watched with anticipation for new delights. I reached into the cooler and took several ice cubes in my hand. "Ali, hold out your hand."

He held out his right hand, and I dropped two ice cubes

into his palm. He jumped slightly and asked, "What is this you have given me?"

"It is frozen water. It will soon melt and become just like the rain."

"An old man in the village told us that one day many years ago such hardened water came from the sky and caused the sheep to run from the pens. How did you get this water from the sky?"

I tried to explain what a refrigerator was but soon gave up when I realized I could not find words to explain how ice was made. Each time I tried to explain, I found myself having to use words that I could not translate into Arabic.

I reached into the cooler and took out two cans of Coke, two sandwiches wrapped in aluminum foil, a bag of potato chips, and two large chocolate chip cookies.

I popped the tabs and showed Ali how to drink from the can. He hesitantly took his first sip. His eyes opened wide, and he spit the Coke out with a sputtering sound.

"This thing you call Coke, it bites my tongue like a pepper. How do you drink it?"

I knew Ali had drunk only water and herbal teas in his short thirteen years. "It will refresh you," I advised as I smiled. I said out loud in English, "I sound like a TV commercial."

Ali looked at me and asked what I had said.

"Oh, nothing important. Here, try some chips. The salt will improve the taste of the Coke."

The aluminum foil was another new experience for Ali. He felt it, wadded it up, and unwrapped it, time after time.

We finished eating, and I said, "Now, we will see if you can use me instead of a bag of rocks."

Just as I spoke, we heard a distant echo resounding in the canyon as the village elder called the third prayer of the day.

His voice sounded eerie as it bounced from one canyon wall to another, growing fainter with each bounce.

"I must pray now." Ali turned and faced north, northwest in the direction of Mecca, the holy city of all Islamites. He stood for a few moments with his eyes upward, then got down on his knees and leaned forward until his forehead touched the ground. He sat back up and leaned over twice more.

When he was finished, I asked him how he knew where Mecca was, since he was away from his village. "I use the sun to tell me," he said simply.

"Now, Ali, it's time to make our first test run." I attached my nylon chest harness rings to the steel clip on the rope's end. With the harness, my body weight would be evenly distributed, making me more comfortable as I hung from the rope.

"Okay, Ali, hold the winch handle in the brake position while I ease over the cliff."

He said nothing, but I could see the concentration on his face.

I sat with my legs hanging over the sheer five-thousand-foot drop. I could not help feeling a slight uneasiness. It reminded me of my first parachute jump. But I did not want Ali to think I was frightened. Like on that first jump, I said to myself, "Here I go." I turned over, faced the cliff, and said softly, "Down, Ali."

I could hear the sound of the winch as the gears meshed . . . clickity clack, clickity clack.

I let go of my handhold on the cliff and felt myself dangling in space. Clickity clack. I went steadily down. I called out, "Stop!" Almost immediately the rope caught tight and held me. I used my feet and hands to keep away from the stony cliff wall. "Good boy, Ali," I shouted.

"Down!" I called, and down I went. Every few feet I used my legs to avoid rough spots where the cliff wall protruded. These spots worried me because the rope could be rubbed ragged against the sharp rock.

I looked around me as I went down. The view was magnificent. Above me the sky was a deep blue with no manmade pollution to mar its beauty. Off to my right the canyon met another canyon, and the two formed a massive chasm that cut the earth for fifty miles.

The rock colors varied from pink to tan to nearly purple with shades of red running horizontally for miles.

About three hundred feet down I decided I was far enough for our first practice effort. I called out, "Up!"

Nothing happened. I called out louder. "Ali, up!"

I felt the rope tighten as Ali started to winch me back up. Suddenly the rope went slack, and with a heart-sickening shock, I fell like a rock. Down, down I went.

7

Ali Saves My Life

SUDDENLY I felt a bone-jarring jerk as I was snapped to a stop. I was hanging upside down, suspended by my harness. For a few moments I just hung there, staring down at the valley floor several thousand feet below.

Regaining my composure, I managed to work myself upright and look up the sheer cliff face. I could see that I had fallen perhaps two hundred feet and that the rope was now taut.

As I was trying to figure out my next move, uncertain if the winch would let go again, I heard Ali's voice calling down to me. "Mr. Wayne, the machine broke. Are you alive?"

I had to laugh. Beyond being bruised from the harness, I was perfectly fine. I looked above me and saw Ali's head, peering over the canyon rim. "Yes, Ali, I am fine. What happened to the machine?"

I knew I was still in great danger. I could drop again if Ali did something wrong.

"The handle that I wind with broke off. The machine let you go, but I stuck the metal rod into the place you showed me, and it stopped moving."

Ali had acted with lightning speed; his quick thinking had saved my life. Now I was more than three hundred feet down the canyon wall with no way up other than to climb, using the rope brakes that I carried. It would be an exhausting process, foot by foot.

"Ali, don't touch the machine. I will have to climb up by hand. Do you understand?"

His small voice came down to me. "Yes, Mr. Wayne, I will not touch the machine."

Shouting that distance was almost as tiring as trying to climb out, so I made a mental note to bring walkie-talkies the next time and teach Ali how to use them.

I took out two rope brakes and attached them to the rope that went from my harness up the cliff. I knew that with the safety rod locking the winch gears, I would have a secure anchor, so I started the climb.

I slid one rope lock up about a foot, locked it, and hoisted myself upward. Then I had to lock the second brake and move the first farther up the rope and lock it again.

For a half hour I repeated the slow and tiring process, gaining about seventy-five feet. My arms ached, and my ribs were sore from the quick stop in the harness. At the rate I was going, I figured it would take me three or four hours to get back up. I shuddered at the thought of not making it to the top before dark.

As I continued to climb, I felt the rope move a little. It went up just a bit, then down. I felt like a yo-yo. I didn't know what was happening. My heart froze at the thought that Ali was trying to fix the winch. If he made a mistake, I could go hurtling down at any moment.

Then, with a slow, steady lift, I was being pulled up the cliff. It was too smooth to be the winch. It did not have the short rope pulsations the winch created with its steel teeth.

"Ali, what is happening?"

There was no answer. I tried again. "Ali, Ali!"

I continued to be moved up, up, up. Whatever was pulling me up was doing a great job. Within five minutes my head was near the cliff edge.

Up, up, up. Suddenly my head rose above the rim, and I was looking out across the grassy slope that led away from the canyon.

In the distance I saw Ali with an Arabian man who was leading a camel. The camel was attached to my rope, pulling while its master was switching it with a small stick. Ali was shouting encouragement to them both.

Neither had seen me come over the canyon edge, and I was still being dragged by the camel. It was such a funny sight that I broke into laughter. I was being dragged across the rocky plateau by a camel, a boy, and a Bedouin.

I stood up and disconnected my snap link, freeing myself from the rope. It was only when the rope suddenly went loose that Ali looked back and saw me. He waved furiously and ran to me as fast as his legs would carry him.

His small face was one big smile as he said, "I saw that Bedouin with his camels, so I asked for his help. We attached the rope, and his camel pulled you up."

"Ali, your quick action and the Bedouin's help may have saved my life! This is a day to remember. Now I want to thank the camel driver."

We walked toward the man and his five camels. When we got to him, he was winding up my rope into a neat circle on the ground.

"Allah be with you, my friend," I said. "You have done me a great service."

The old Bedouin had a face like leather with deep creases running from his nose to his chin. He was dressed in a dark foot-length robe and wore a black head cover held in place by a leather band. Over one shoulder he carried a long leather belt, heavy with tarnished brass bullets. In his black waist tie he carried a sharply curved dagger with a horn handle that was trimmed with gold. He reached out his hand to me and bowed his head slightly.

"I greet you in the name of Allah and the people of my tribe. When this young man told me of your situation, I was pleased to help."

"I am deeply in your debt. Thank you for the help," I said.

"I can see you are a Westerner. Are you English?"

"No, I am an American. I live in the walled compound about fifteen kilometers that way," I said, pointing.

The old Bedouin squinted as he looked in the direction I was pointing. "Ah, yes, I know the place. It is where the big noise comes from. I do not like that noise; it bothers our sheep and goats when we graze them nearby."

I knew the man was talking about the diesel generator that ran twenty-four hours a day to supply electricity for our camp. The quiet stillness of the desert was broken by the loud sound of the big generator, but it was something that had to be. Our camp was thirty miles from the nearest Arabian town, but the wandering desert Bedouins, with their mobile tent camps, often set up housekeeping nearby to let their animals graze on the green grass created by our camp's water runoff.

"One day we will leave the desert, and your animals will graze in peace again," I assured him.

"As Allah wills it. Now I must be on my way," he answered as he switched his camels into a trot.

"Thanks again for your help," I shouted above the soft thunder of camel's feet.

"Mr. Wayne, I do not know what happened to the machine, but it made a noise and started running fast."

"Let's go see what went wrong, Ali."

As I examined the winch, I saw that the crank handle had broken at the weld, leaving Ali nothing with which to control my descent. Ali had done the only thing that could stop my fall by pushing the safety rod into the wheel cogs, stopping them from meshing.

"I need to take this to the place I live to get it fixed, Ali. Would you like to come along?"

"Oh, yes, that would be fine."

"Okay, let's go!" I removed the crank handle from the winch mechanism and threw it into the back of the Rover.

"Ali, you're going to see many new things today," I said as we drove across the plateau toward the compound.

After about five miles we came to a dusty road that led to the paved route from Abha to Khamis Mushayt.

As I drove onto the main road, there was a big tanker truck roaring down the highway. Ali's eyes widened as he saw the big gas rig speeding toward us.

"What is that?" he asked in amazement.

"That is a truck. It carries fuel to feed the other cars and trucks you will see today."

"Tra—traaaa—" he tried.

"Truck, Ali. Truck," I repeated.

"Truck. Truck. Truck," he said.

"That's it. Now you have it."

As we drove, several cars passed in both directions, each filled with Arabian men with their white clothing blowing in the wind. Ali looked at everything carefully. Much of what he was seeing was for the first time.

At one point a Bedouin family with dozens of camels and hundreds of sheep and goats was crossing the road. Half a dozen cars were stopped, waiting for the road to clear, but all were patient as the tribespeople herded their animals. The Arabian people were well aware that within the space of a few years they had come from being an underdeveloped, poor country to the threshold of becoming a wealthy modern monarchy.

People who had ridden camels and herded sheep last year now drove cars and trucks and built cities with the help of various companies from all over the world. Money earned from exporting oil was making Saudi Arabia the wealthiest country in the world. Except for people from remote villages like Ali's, life had changed dramatically for Saudi citizens.

I turned off on a dirt road and drove toward the walled compound sitting on a hill in the distance. As we approached the gates, an old Arab swung them open to let me pass. He waved at me and smiled a toothless grin.

"That's Abdullah, our gatekeeper. He and one other Arabian work here during the day," I told Ali.

The compound was composed of twenty-two stucco houses and two larger buildings that housed the dining hall and the recreation center. A concrete wall, nine feet high, completely enclosed the area. It kept out the roving bands of baboons and other wild animals drawn by the smell of food.

"Here we are, Ali. This is where I live," I said as we got out of the vehicle.

He looked around at the buildings and cars parked in the lots. His eyes said it all. "Mr. Wayne, what is this? What is that?" Ali was curious and full of questions. I answered and explained the function of various things. His biggest thrill was when I touched the light switch in my quarters.

He blinked in amazement. "It is all too much for me to understand," he said.

"In time, Ali, it will all seem perfectly natural to you," I assured him.

As we walked outside, he looked at the houses and at a row of vans parked in front of the dining hall.

"That is where we eat. Come, let's see what there is left over from lunch."

The chef, a black giant of a man from Sudan, with tribal scars etched into his cheeks, was cooking dinner with his two Korean helpers. He smiled to me and called out from the kitchen, "Who's your new friend, boss?"

"This is Ali, son of Mustafa from the village of Ezratu, down in the canyon."

Switching to Arabic, the Sudanese called, "Welcome, Ali. Would you like something to eat?"

Still looking at everything in wonder and amazement, Ali said, "Yes, I am very hungry."

"Well then, sit down and I'll bring you today's special. It's curried chicken and rice with raisins, coconut, nuts, and pineapple garnish."

Ali didn't have the faintest idea of what the chef was talking about, but he was ready for whatever there was to eat.

Soon we were served plates of steaming chicken in a fragrant curry sauce heaped over a bed of rice. The fruit and nut garnishes were generously sprinkled over the top.

Ali placed his left hand on his lap and started eating with his right hand, using his fingers instead of a fork.

"Here, like this," I said as I picked up a fork and started eating.

Ali picked up his fork and tried. At first he stuck himself in the lip, but he soon got the hang of it.

After eating a second helping, Ali put down his fork and said, "Never have I eaten anything so delicious."

The big Sudanese chef heard Ali and made a sweeping bow. We all laughed.

I took Ali to the company workshop, where two Korean

mechanics were hard at work on a Dodge van. I showed them my broken crank handle and asked if they could make another one, but stronger.

They both stopped working on the task at hand to make me a new handle. As they turned on the welding torch, Ali watched every step. The men did not speak Arabic but smiled broadly and let Ali hold the torch for a moment. Ali waved it around and laughed loudly. "There is so much to see and learn in the world. I must tell my father and brothers about everything."

I left Ali with the mechanics to watch them make the handle while I gathered up some more equipment. When the strong new crank handle was finished, we drove back to the canyon.

It was late afternoon when we got back. I fixed the winch, wound the rope back onto the spool, and examined the whole thing for other defects. It looked perfect.

To preclude having to drive all the way back to the compound to sleep, I had brought along a three-man tent, some sleeping bags, a camp stove, and some canned food. I had also picked up two walkie-talkies from the camp. I planned to sleep on the plateau and asked Ali if he wished to spend the night on the rim rather than make the tiring climb back down.

Just as he was about to speak, the call to prayer echoed from the village below. Ali got down and did his evening ritual prayer, then stood on the rim and called down. "This is Ali, son of Mustafa. I will not return this night. Tell my father I am well."

When the echoes subsided, a distant voice called back, "As Allah wills it, Ali. I will tell your father." It was one of the night shepherds near the cliff face who heard the message and called back.

I showed Ali how to pitch the tent, started the camp stove, and cooked an old American favorite, beans from a can with hot applesauce on the side.

The blackness of night was complete when we finished eating. Overhead the stars shone with brilliant intensity, and a cold night wind made me pull my jacket collar close.

Ali and I sat and talked for two hours, with the flames of a campfire keeping us warm. I told him about America and Europe. I explained how King Khalid ruled over all Saudi Arabia and how the village of Ezratu was one of hundreds that made up the country. I was relating a story about the king when I noticed Ali was quiet. I looked across the firelight to see him fast asleep. I picked him up, carried him into the tent, and covered him with an unzipped sleeping bag.

I went back out and crawled into my own bag under the stars. The night was cold, and the air was sharp, but the clarity of the night sky was too much to miss.

The night sounds faded as I snuggled deep into my bag. Tomorrow would come soon enough.

8

The Eagle's Nest

"It is a new day! Wake up!" Ali was excited, bright-eyed and ready to begin our search for a baby eagle.

I looked at my watch. It was six-thirty. I felt stiff from the hard ground, and my hips were sore from sleeping with them pressed against the rocky soil, but the dawn was so beautiful I had to smile as I did a big stretch.

Ali was saying his morning prayers, and I saw how intense he was. He believed in God without reservation, and it colored his every word and action.

When Saudi Arabians gave their word, it was better than all the written contracts in the world. They prayed as a nation, and they were their brothers' keepers. I was learning much from these desert people.

We had a simple breakfast of pita bread, canned corned beef hash, and canned fruit cocktail.

After we put the camping gear in the Rover, I set up the winch, checked it again, and prepared my harness. I had a strong canvas bag with several holes cut in it for air. If all went well, I would return with a baby eagle in it.

"Ali, this is a walkie-talkie. I want you to watch closely

while I show you how to work it." I showed him how to push the transmit button, talk, and then release to listen.

I walked several hundred yards across the desert and stopped. "Ali, can you hear me?" I spoke into the mike.

After a moment's pause Ali's voice came over my radio. "It is like magic, Mr. Wayne. You are in this little box!"

"Just my voice is in the box, Ali. So is yours, in my box."

With the test complete, I went back to the hoist and Ali. We went over the commands twice more, but I could see that my young friend was way ahead of me. "Okay, it's time for me to go down the cliff face."

I snapped on my harness, clicked the snap locks onto the rope, and adjusted the straps to fit comfortably. I made sure the rope was threaded through the pulley, then cranked the winch tension until the rope was tight from my harness to the crank.

Ali took his place at the winch while I eased over the side, using the rope to hold myself. "Okay, Ali, start me down. When I want to talk to you, I will use the walkie-talkie."

Clickity clack, clickity clack. The gears meshed, and I started down the wall.

It was seven-twenty in the morning, a time when the eagle chicks would be hungry from a night without food. I was banking that both the mother and the father eagles would be away hunting when I reached the nest.

Down, down I went, using my feet to bounce off the wall. Several times I made radio checks with Ali, and he answered.

Below me, on a rocky outcrop, I could see a large area whitened by years of falling eagle guano. I began to get excited as I dropped nearer the ledge where the white began.

"Stop, Ali!"

The rope stopped. I was about twenty feet above the ledge. I looked and listened for signs of the eagles. Just as I was watching, an adult eagle flew out into the cool morning air.

I remained motionless, hoping it would not see me. It dropped like a diver bomber with its wings tucked, hurtling toward the valley floor, several thousand feet below. Then another eagle flew out and stayed high as it proceeded farther out into the canyon before diving for the bottom.

"Whew, that was close," I said to myself. A moment sooner, and I would have been at their doorstep face-to-beak with the two large eagles.

I keyed the radio mike and softly said, "Okay, Ali, let me down slowly and be ready to stop in just a moment."

"As you wish," replied Ali.

The rope started down again. I used my hands and feet to work my way toward the ledge from which I had seen the eagles fly. My position was about fifteen feet too far from the ledge so I would have to swing over to it once I was at its level.

"Stop!"

The rope stopped. I grasped a cleft in the rock and held fast. To get across to the rock ledge, I would have to swing like a clock pendulum, grab the ledge, get onto it, and secure myself before I looked for the eagle chicks.

"Ali, keep the winch locked until I tell you to give me some more rope. Then give me two turns and lock it again."

"As you wish, Mr. Wayne."

I was amazed at his calm and confident response.

I took a breath, let go, and pushed myself off to the right. I swung out a few feet and then came right back. I pushed harder and swung even farther. Twice more I kept up the momentum. At the end of the arc I saw a narrow ledge, about ten inches wide, sticking out from the vertical wall. I reached out for it and grabbed. My fingers slipped off, and I swung back to the other end.

"Down," I radioed to Ali. I dropped about a foot as I swung back toward the ledge. "Stop!"

Again I reached for the ledge, and this time I held on. I placed my right leg over the ledge. For a moment I thought I was going to make it, but I slipped off and dropped in a falling arc.

"Up," I radioed. The rope went up.

"Stop!" The rope stopped.

I made one more big swing and reached out for the ledge, this time from above.

Success! I grabbed an indentation in the stone and held fast. I reached my feet down and cautiously stood on the ledge. I was face-to-face with the canyon wall, my nose pressed against the stone.

"Ali, let me down just a little, but don't stop until I say so."

"Okay."

I smiled as I heard him use the American expression *okay*.

The rope eased, and as my eyes passed over the upper edge of the crevice, I saw that the recess went back about seven feet.

"Stop." The rope stopped.

I leaned into the cave entrance and started to crawl in. There before my eyes was a large eagle nest made from sticks and leaves. It was padded with feathers and smelled awful. Backed against the rocky cave wall, it was at least six feet across from edge to edge.

I slowly crawled over to the nest. As I peered into it, a sudden shrill shriek and explosive movement made me jump back. There were two chicks in the nest, one larger than the other.

The larger one had opened its sharply pointed beak and hissed at me. I was amazed at how big the chick was, bigger than some of the full-grown falcons I had seen in Ali's village.

I crawled back again. The baby eagles watched me with small, bright eyes. I reached into my pocket and pulled out leather gloves and put them on. I opened the canvas bag and kept my eyes on the eagles, trying to figure out how to get one into the bag.

I decided to try for the smaller of the two. But I would have to get by the big guy first.

"Ali, I am at the eagle's nest. I am going to try to catch one. When I say up, wind as fast as you can."

"Okay. I will be ready."

I zipped up my jacket all the way, turned the collar up, and moved to the side where the smaller bird was. I could see piles of stringy bones littering the nest bottom. No wonder it smelled so bad.

"Okay, little bird, let's go for a ride." I held the bag wide open and made a quick motion to slip it over the eagle chick. He was twice as fast as I was and jumped across the nest to stand on the edge. The larger chick hissed at me and kept reaching out with its beak, clicking in the air.

"Well, that won't work. Let's see what will." I was talking to both myself and the chicks.

Keeping my eye on the big chick, I crawled into the nest and reached for the smaller bird's legs. As I did, it slashed fiercely at my gloved hand. The larger chick was flapping its wings, stirring up feathers and dust while it attacked my left shoulder.

I caught the chick's leg, but it fought strongly, trying to get away. Then I got its other leg. I pulled it toward me across the rough nest bottom. It flapped its wings and hissed angrily.

It was bedlam. I struggled with the bird, trying to get its

wings folded so I could shove it into the bag. Finally I was able to lift the bird up and push it headfirst into the bag. The moment I closed the drawstring, it quieted down.

The other chick was standing with its wings open like a flag ornament, hissing with its black, pointed tongue out. I quickly backed up to the cave opening. I turned around so I could see out and prepared to let myself back onto the rope's support.

I cradled the eagle closely and tied a short rope around the neck of the bag. I then slung it over my shoulder like Santa with a bag of toys. I needed my hands free to get back up, and I did not want to crush the bird between my body and the cliff wall.

"Okay, Ali, I have the eagle and I am leaving the cave. Keep the rope locked until I swing out."

"Do you really have the bird? Allah be praised!"

I heard it before I saw it. One of the adult eagles was folding its wings in flight to slow down for a landing. I turned and saw it less than ten feet from me. It was a sight so beautiful I almost forget the danger it posed.

I had to act *now*!

I jumped out into space, "Up, Ali, up! Fast as you can," I called.

The rope started upward. I knew little Ali would have to use all his strength to get my two hundred pounds plus the eagle up to the rim.

The parent eagle whistled as it wheeled in flight. From within my bag the baby whistled back.

"Uh-oh," I said out loud. "Mama knows I have her baby."

I was moving up the wall at a steady pace while the big eagle kept flying at me, trying to see where the chick was.

Foot by foot I went up. Five hundred feet, four hundred; we were making progress.

Then the eagle must have heard her other chick calling, and she flew to her nest below.

Finally I was within sight of the rim.

"Ali, I'm just below, so wind slowly and stop me just at the rim so I can hand you the bag with the chick."

When my face appeared over the rim, Ali stopped and locked the gear. I pulled the bag from my shoulder and handed it to him. When he held it safely, I crawled over the top and sat down.

I was nearly exhausted, but we had what we had come for. The chick struggled in the bag, but Ali spoke to it softly. "Little eagle, you and I will become the best of friends. I will take good care of you and feed you well."

Ali looked at me and laughed happily, "Oh, Mr. Wayne, today is the best day of my whole life."

Watching Ali, sitting there holding the bag with the baby eagle in it and listening to his fervent words, I knew it all had been worth it.

"This has been one of the best days of my life, too, Ali."

After packing the climbing gear in the Rover, I carefully placed the eagle in its sack on some folded sleeping bags to keep it comfortable and safe until we could get it to the village.

We drove around the rim and stopped directly above the village. "Okay, let's get this big bird to its new home," I said as I opened the door of the Rover.

"My father and my brothers will be very surprised when they see what I have in the bag. This will show my oldest brother, Faud. He always picks on me when our father is away. His mother is senior to mine, so he treats me as if I were his personal slave."

I knew a long climb down the rocks would endanger the eagle, so I quickly set up the frame and winch and attached all the rope I had. If I figured it right, it would reach the bottom with a little to spare.

"Ali, I'm going to lower you and the eagle down the rope so we can be sure we don't hurt it."

"Okay, Mr. Wayne."

I was starting to buckle Ali into his harness when I realized he had spoken to me in English. He saw my look of surprise and laughed with pleasure.

Within minutes I had Ali and his eagle halfway to the canyon floor. I looked to check the remaining rope and knew we would make it all the way.

In fifteen minutes his feet were on the ground, and I started down. When I reached the bottom, Ali was waiting for me. "Let us hurry. I can't wait to see the eagle. I have been telling it all about my father and the village and what a wonderful life it will have living with us in this valley. Also, I can't wait to see the look on Faud's face when I open the bag."

"Okay, Ali, it's been a long day. We will hurry. I can't wait to see your father's face when you bring him your big surprise."

9

Ali's Big Surprise

"FATHER! FATHER, come quickly!" Ali shouted as we neared his house.

His voice carried down the rocky street, bringing curious eyes to many windows.

Mustafa was sitting on the house's flat roof when he heard Ali's shout. "Well," he called down, "my son the great traveler and our American friend are back. Come to the roof!"

Ali rushed ahead of me into the main entrance. His mother, Najid, was preparing the evening meal.

"Ali, slow down and do not run in the house," she scolded. When she saw me, she paused and looked, uncertain of what to do.

I smiled and nodded in greeting.

"Mother, I have the best surprise ever. It's right here in this bag."

Najid looked at the big bag over her son's shoulder, saw it moving, and asked, "Did you catch a fox?"

Ali's eyes lit up as he smiled and said, "Mother, come to

the roof with me to see Father. Then you will see what I have."

Najid, Mustafa's youngest wife, mother of Ali and his brother Raman, hesitated. Though she had been a wife to Mustafa for fourteen years, she still came last in line to his other two wives, who were busy nearby and listening to Ali's excited plea.

Najid knew she must not go to Mustafa unless the other two agreed. As she looked their way, both nodded with silent smiles that told her she could go up to him.

As Ali and I hurried up the winding, dusty staircase within the square tower of the house, Najid demurely followed. She loved both her sons and her three daughters, but I could see Ali held a special place in her heart.

Mustafa had told me about Najid and her "favorite" son when we had talked late into the night on a previous visit. He said Ali reminded her of her father, an energetic man who had been the chief in her village of Sabya. She had been sold to Mustafa when she was fourteen, for ten sheep, four goats, and a ram. In the tradition of her people, she became his third wife, joining two older wives who had already borne him two sons and seven daughters.

Mustafa had told me that Ali was special to him as well. The village seeress had predicted that Ali, born the night of a full moon, at the height of Ramadan, the Islamic month of fasting, would grow up to become a great leader.

It was obvious to everyone in the village that from the first moment Ali was the light of his father's eye. During the succeeding years Mustafa had trained his sons in the skills of hunting and survival but always paid more attention to Ali than to the others.

This caused much jealousy among his older brothers, who

each vied to be their father's favorite. It often led to an older brother's going out of his way to make Ali look bad.

Now, as Ali burst onto the roof and stood in the midst of his brothers seated in a half circle at Mustafa's feet, he proudly held his bag in front of him.

"Welcome, Wayne. Please sit here," Mustafa said, gesturing to a place near him. "Well, Ali, what is so exciting that you have to shout for all the village to hear?"

Ali took a deep breath, smiled his broadest grin, and announced: "Father, Mr. Wayne and I have caught an eagle baby!"

"What?" exclaimed Mustafa. "Really? You have caught an eagle?"

"Yes, Father, we have it in this bag."

"By the beard of Muhammad, Wayne, is it possible?"

Mustafa's mind was racing because no one in their valley had ever caught an eagle. He knew the word would spread to every village in the great canyon rift.

"Should I take it out of the bag?"

"No, son. No! Come with me. We will go to the falcon roost and do this thing right."

"May we come, Father?" asked one of Ali's half brothers.

"Yes, everyone come. We will see what kind of bird Ali and Mr. Wayne have brought us."

The wives and sisters watched as Mustafa, his sons, and I hurried toward the aviary. As we walked, Ali's brothers called to their friends along the way, "We have an eagle. Come and see."

The group grew as we passed each house along the way and were joined by curious onlookers.

At the falcon roost Mustafa carefully opened the door so as not to frighten the other birds on their perches. It was near dark inside, so Mustafa asked his oldest son, Faud, to light torches. When the torches were glowing brightly, at least thirty people crowded into the low building, many stationing themselves near their own hunting birds.

"Ali, place the bag here on the trimming table."

As the others watched in awe, Ali lifted the heavy bag and carefully placed it on the table. I stood back with Ali's brothers and watched while Mustafa wrapped his hands with toughened goatskin and placed a wicker face mask over his head.

"Now let's see what we have," he said as he untied the bag and carefully reached in to try to find the bird's feet so that he could bring it out.

Suddenly he withdrew his hand with blood running from a tear in the leather hand cover and cried, "By the grace of Allah, this bird has the strength of a burro."

Laughter ran through the room until Mustafa glowered at the surrounding onlookers. The room fell silent again.

After wrapping another layer of leather around his hands, Mustafa again reached into the bag. Everybody watched intently as he struggled to get the eagle out. Finally, amid a shower of feathers, the eagle was pulled out feet first, flapping its big wings furiously.

A cheer arose, followed by a hushed awe as the group saw the size of the young bird. It was fully twice as large as the biggest falcon in the building, and it was not half grown.

"This bird is magnificent! Look at the chick feathers still mixed with the flight feathers. This bird cannot be more than ten weeks old, and it is already so huge."

"This is the first time I have seen it, Father. Mr. Wayne told me the reason this chick was not killed by the other, older chick was that it was so large and strong."

"You must tell us how this mighty bird was caught. I will call a village meeting for tomorrow."

"Father, I have seen things you will not believe while I was up on the top of the cliff. Mr. Wayne took me in what he calls a jeep that drinks foul-smelling liquid. We went with the wind . . . Oh, there is so much to tell."

"We are anxious to hear all about it, son, but now let us make this big bird a proper roost. We will have to learn how to keep this eagle happy and train it to like us."

As he spoke, Mustafa snapped a metal ring onto the eagle's left leg and then attached a heavy leather thong to it. He let the eagle go, and it immediately tried to fly but was held back by the thong.

"Ali, if we can master this bird, we will have the greatest hunter in all Arabia, perhaps in all the world. There is a long road ahead, but we will take it together."

Ali looked at his father's serious face, and their eyes met.

"Son, today, you have acted as a man. I will ask the village elders to give you the test of manhood. Normally the test would not take place until your fourteenth birthday, but you have proved you are a man by climbing the great wall and bringing back this eagle. Since your birthday is near, I'm sure there won't be any problem in holding your test a little early. Unless someone has an objection, the official ceremony will take place at the end of the week."

There was mumbling and nodding of heads as everyone in the room agreed.

"Now, if everyone will please leave except for Ali, Faud, and Wayne, we can get started taking care of this new addition to our aviary."

Amid dust stirred up from their tramping feet, the others

left, leaving Mustafa, his oldest and youngest sons, and me in the building.

Working with wood from thorn trees, gathered from the valley, we built a heavy perch and placed it at the far end of the building. It stood about four feet high and was topped with a horizontal, rounded perch bar for the eagle to stand on.

When we were finished, Mustafa stood behind the perch and pulled the thong on the eagle's foot until it opened its wings and flapped up and onto the bar. He securely tied the leather to the bar and stood back.

The young eagle tried its wings but was held by the tether. It pulled its leg violently, trying to get free, was held fast, then, with a slash of its sharp downturned beak, bit the leather in two and was loose.

"Ali, close the door! Faud, get a head cover," shouted Mustafa as he tried to catch the frantic bird.

Hopping and fluttering, the eagle struggled to be free. Then, in a fury of flapping wings, unsuccessful in an attempt to fly, the eagle jumped onto a falcon's perch. The falcon lashed out with its beak, striking the young bird on the right wing root.

Blood flowed down the dark feathers as the bird hesitated a moment while the falcon struck again. This time the eagle moved with lightning speed, causing the falcon to miss its bite. Almost faster than the eye could see, the eagle raised itself on fluttering wings and grabbed the falcon with both sets of talons. When the bird closed its feet, its talons knifed into the smaller bird, puncturing its body.

The eagle dropped to the dirt floor and savagely bit into the falcon. It was over in ten seconds. The ten-week-old eagle had killed an adult hunting falcon before Mustafa or his sons could stop it.

"We will have to catch this bird in the dark!" shouted Mustafa. "Wait until I get ready; then put out all the torches except the small one in the far corner. . . . Now! Snuff out the torches."

Both boys did as instructed; the light went out.

Feeling his way across the floor, Mustafa carefully located the eagle. When Mustafa's hand touched its leg, it raked at him with its beak. "Ow! . . ." he shouted.

He reached again, got a leg and then the other. He pulled the legs back until the bird was on its chest in the dirt. Mustafa placed a heavy leather hood over the bird's head and lashed its feet together with an extra-heavy leather strap that had been hardened by being dried in salt water.

"Light the torches!" Ali took the charcoal ember and started the torches again. There stood Mustafa, with the big bird hanging upside down from his bloody hands.

"Now, my eagle friend, we shall see who is master of this aviary. Faud, fasten half an arm's length of chain to the perch, and then stand back."

After the chain was fastened, Mustafa carefully linked the eagle's leg iron to the chain and then raised the bird and set its feet on the perch. Its sharp talons grabbed hold, and it was still.

"Father, I am sorry that the eagle killed one of the falcons. I will offer to work for the owner for a week to make up for it."

"Yes, that would be just, Ali. Now we all deserve some dinner and a good night's rest."

Secure on its perch, the eagle remained quiet. The other birds were still restless, but when the room was in darkness again, they, too, settled down.

The night sky was black as pitch when we left the aviary. Looking up, we saw stars shimmering like distant beacons as we returned to the house. We enjoyed a large dinner, then went to bed. This time a bed had been prepared for me in the big room where Mustafa's sons slept. To be accepted as "family" was considered an honor.

A few minutes later, when Ali was nearly asleep, I saw Mustafa go to Ali's bed and sit on the floor next to him. I heard him say, "Together we will train this eagle, and it will become the master of the sky. Good-night, my son. Sleep with Allah's peace."

10

Ali Faces a Lion

THE NEXT MORNING I woke up to find all the boys gone from their beds. I heard the family downstairs talking, so I went down and was greeted by a very happy Mustafa. He smiled broadly and took my hand in a leathery grip. He winced slightly, from the pain of the eagle bite he suffered the night before.

"Come, let's see how the eagle is this morning. Ali went to him before dawn."

Mustafa led the way, past the other birds on their perches, to the far end of the building.

Then I saw Ali and the eagle. It was eating a piece of red meat Ali had given it, holding the meat down with its talons while it ripped off pieces with its sharp beak.

"That meat comes from an old burro that I killed because it was lame. Only Ali will feed the eagle. The bird has several moons to grow before we can start its real training, but we will start its exercises immediately. It is important that the eagle never fear us. It must trust the hand that feeds it and respect its trainer."

"Mustafa, can you tell what sex the eagle is?" I asked.

"It is a male," he replied matter-of-factly. "You may have the honor of giving it a name. What shall we call him?"

I thought and thought. A dozen names went through my head, in both Arabic and English.

I looked at the eagle. He was big and shaggy because his chick pinfeathers were still being replaced by adult flight feathers. He looked tough with his turned-down beak and dark, shining eyes.

Suddenly I had it, the perfect name. "Mustafa, Ali, meet Samson."

Mustafa smiled and repeated the name with an Arabic inflection. "Som-soon."

"Close enough, my friend, Samson it is."

Ali, who had learned a few words in English, repeated the name perfectly: "Samson."

We spent half an hour with the eagle and several of the other birds before Mustafa announced: "My sons and I have to tend the fields today. Ali must tend the flock on the high slope above the village. You are welcome to go with him if you like."

It was a gorgeous day as Ali and I walked up the rocky path toward the grazing area. The air in the valley was dry and cool enough to see our breaths. We came upon a flock of about 150 sheep and goats tended by a boy who looked no older than nine or ten. He smiled as we approached. "There has been an old female lion watching the flock since this morning. She took a sheep before I could scare her away. I fear the old lion is still around, Ali, so be on the alert," he said.

"I will take care of the old lion, Mestusus. Go home now and eat," Ali replied.

The boy handed Ali his crooked staff, said hello and good-bye to me, and trotted off.

Again I was awed by the strength of character of these boys, who let nothing, not even a marauding lion, interfere with their duties.

Ali walked among the animals, counting quietly to himself. As he counted, he called out friendly greetings to some of the newborns nursing at their mother's sides. "Good morning, little one. Watch out for that bad old lion. Ali will protect you."

He stopped and examined several sheep like a doctor with patients. He felt their stomachs, looked into their mouths, and inspected their ears.

The day warmed as the rays of the sun crept from behind the canyon wall. The village was so deep in the canyon the sun's direct rays shone on it only from about eleven in the morning to three in the afternoon. After that the sun was behind the canyon rim, out of sight but still lighting the deep chasm.

Ali and I passed the time talking as he kept a watchful eye on the herd. By five the shadows of evening were making the valley floor dark. Ali would be relieved by the night shepherd, an older boy of seventeen, at last light.

Several sheep stirred on the far side of the herd. The lead ram trotted over to see what was the matter. Suddenly we both saw tawny blur as a lion leaped from the high rock and landed in the midst of the herd. Sheep and goats scattered, bleating in panic. Without a word, Ali leaped up and ran directly toward the lion. As he ran, he reached down and grabbed two stones. The lion already had a full-grown sheep pinned to the ground and was trying to break its neck.

Thirty feet from the lion Ali placed one of the rocks into his sling and spun his arm above his head. Swish, swish, the leather sling straps hummed as they bit the air.

Ali dropped his wrist and let the first stone fly. Thunk! It hit the lion squarely on its rib cage. It looked up and let the sheep fall.

Ali placed the second stone in his sling and whirled his arm again. Thunk! The stone caught the animal right between the eyes. It swatted at the pain with a big paw. Now, about fifteen feet away, Ali picked up another stone and put it into the sling. The big cat started moving slowly toward Ali and crouched, ready to spring.

I recognized the danger Ali was in, but I had no weapon and was at a loss at what to do.

Ali's arm whirled, and he let the stone fly. I heard a soft, splatlike sound as the stone hit the lion right on its nose. The big cat let out a growl and pawed at its nose. Shouting furiously, Ali suddenly jumped forward. The lion had had enough. It turned and ran, gathering speed as it went.

Ali shouted after it, "Go eat somewhere else. These sheep are not for you."

I watched the scene completely unbelieving. Like some biblical David, this thirteen-year-old boy had faced a lion three times his own size and won.

"Ali! That was the bravest thing I have ever seen!" I exclaimed.

"The old lion comes here from time to time, and we lose some sheep, but it must eat, too. I am always careful not to hit it too hard, just enough to scare it away."

"Do you mean you've done this before?" I asked.

"Many times, Mr. Wayne. Each of the shepherds has to face the lions. There are very few of them left, so it is always a special day when one is seen."

"Ali, you have taught me much today. I like your valley and the ways of your people more each time I visit here."

"Is it better than your world where machines fly?" he asked.

"Yes, Ali, in some ways it is much better." The beauty and naturalness of the canyon people, along with their strength of character, were something I had never found in all my world travels.

By sunset the relief shepherd had arrived, and after Ali had warned him about the lion, we started down the slope to the village.

As we walked, Ali explained the coming-of-age ceremony that was to take place the next day. "It will last all day and into the night," he concluded.

"Are you a little frightened about the ceremony, Ali?" I asked.

"Yes, Mr. Wayne, I am, but I must make my father proud."

11

Ali Comes of Age

THE DAWN was sharply colder than the day before. A chill from the stone floor made my bones ache and my muscles stiff. As I sat up from my bed of hay, I looked out the open window to see the rugged brown gullies of the dry washes.

I could hear many voices from the street below, so I stiffly crawled up to see what was happening. To my surprise, men *and* women were on the streets.

An even bigger surprise, the women were not dressed in their black chadors. They still wore veils that hid their features, but they had on colorful clothes, and rows of gold bracelets sparkled and jangled on their arms.

"Boy, this coming-of-age thing must be a big event," I said out loud.

I found myself alone in the big sleeping room. On a table sat a wooden bowl of water for me to wash in. I rinsed my face with the refreshing cold liquid and splashed some on my bare chest.

Just then two of Ali's brothers came in. "Mr. Wayne, our father asks that you join him in the eating room below. Ali is being kept in another house until the ceremony begins."

I grabbed my shirt and jacket. I slipped my arms into the shirtsleeves, buttoned it, and followed them down to the eating room.

Mustafa was seated on a heavy hand-carved stool by a table made of a gnarled piece of wood, supported by three limbs in their natural state. "Allah's blessing, Wayne. This is a wonderful day. It is the day my youngest son takes the vows of manhood. Because of the eagle, the village elders have voted that you can take part. Our women will be with us today, and you will see why we keep them covered up; they are the most beautiful women in all Arabia. Come, share food with me."

We all ate in silence, but the two half brothers kept looking at each other as if they were sharing a secret. I wondered why they were so quiet.

After we had finished eating, I went with Mustafa to a rock-strewn clearing in the middle of the village where a wooden platform had been erected with rows of benches all around it.

Dressed in festive attire, the people were wandering toward the platform, chattering excitedly. Men, women, and children, some with their dogs, came from every house.

"Sit here, my friend," said Mustafa, pointing to a low stumplike seat close to the platform.

I sat down.

The village women were staring at me from behind dark veils. When I looked back, they suddenly shifted their eyes away. Many giggled softly as they talked among themselves. I guess I was something of a curiosity with my light skin and hair, Levi's jeans, and leather jacket.

Within minutes everyone in the village had gathered around the platform. Suddenly all the chattering ceased. A bent-over old man with an animal-skin cape draped around his shoulders hobbled up to the center of the platform. He looked a hundred years old. His face was like worn leather, deeply etched with dozens of creases and marked by numerous scars.

Very quietly Mustafa whispered, "He is the wisest, most powerful imam in the whole valley. He can see into the future. No one dares challenge his wisdom."

The holy man raised both arms, revealing a bony chest covered with scars and tattoos. He held a knobby wooden staff in his right hand, and turning in four directions, he mumbled something I did not understand.

No one spoke a word.

In a gravelly voice the imam shouted, "Bring on the boy!"

From a mud and stone hut built against the rocky stone wall of the canyon, two men walked toward the assembled villagers with Ali between them. He was dressed in a white robe and wore leather sandals. On his head was a dark band, holding his hair back. He looked different somehow. As the three reached the platform, the two men stopped.

The imam gestured with his staff for Ali to join him. He slowly climbed the dusty steps to the platform. A murmur ran through the crowd as the imam reached out to place his hand on Ali's head.

I listened as he spoke in a crackly, low voice. He kept one hand on Ali's head and held his staff high with the other. "Today Ali, son of Mustafa, of the village Ezratu, will be tested for manhood. If he passes the tests, he will henceforth be considered a man. He will hunt as a man, work as a man, and be able to take a wife as a man. If he should fail, he will be sent back to his father's house to live as a boy until another year has passed. To fail the manhood test brings disgrace on himself and his father's house."

The imam called orders to a man who was stoking a fire

near the platform. The man reached for the wooden handle of a metal rod that was protruding from the red-hot coals, walked to the platform, and handed it to the imam.

"This test is for pain. A man does not flinch as his flesh is burned." He showed the glowing red iron to the crowd. There was a hushed mumblings.

I looked at the back rows where the women sat and saw Ali's mother and sisters. His mother was trying to be brave as her son faced extreme pain, but I could see that like any mother, she would have liked to protect him. However, if she uttered one word or screamed out, Ali's manhood ritual would be canceled.

"Ali, bare your chest," ordered the imam.

Ali dropped his robe and tucked it in so he was bare from the waist up.

The imam lowered the hot iron with smoke curling from its tip. He slowly placed it near Ali's chest. Just an inch away he stopped. By the look in his eyes I could see Ali was scared.

"Wayne," whispered Mustafa, "we were all as frightened as Ali when we went through this. Do you have such tests for your young men in America?"

I was watching the hot iron poised near Ali as I listened to Mustafa. I wondered what a thirteen-year-old American boy would do in Ali's place.

"No, Mustafa, we do not have such a ritual for our passage to manhood," I answered.

The imam placed the hot iron on Ali's bare skin just above his heart. Sssssst. A wisp of smoke rose where Ali's skin was burned. Ali's face twitched, but he remained motionless and silent.

"Ahhhhh." The crowd was pleased. They watched the iron held flush against Ali and saw that he was not going to cry out.

It lasted only two seconds. Then the iron was taken away.

For a full two minutes the imam stood face-to-face with Ali, as if waiting to see what he would do. Then he took Ali's face in his hands and kissed each of his cheeks. He raised his staff toward the sky and shouted: "Ali has passed the first test!"

A cheer, led by Mustafa, arose from the audience. I noticed Ali's two half brothers were not joining in. I could not help wondering about these two boys' lack of support for their brother's victory over pain.

The imam took a bowl with a salve in it and smeared it on Ali's burn. "Let the next test begin!" he called.

My heart hurt for my young friend, despite the fact that I knew this was a ritual that had been going on for centuries.

A man carried a wicker basket onto the platform, sat it down, then hurried away.

"Now for the test of courage!" shouted the imam. He took the lid off the basket and quickly stepped back.

Mustafa leaned over to whisper to me, explaining the next test. "In the basket is a large cobra. Its bite can kill in five minutes. Ali must touch the snake without being bitten. If he moves slowly and keeps his eyes on the snake, he can do it. We have lost young men in this test, one during last year's ceremony."

I desperately wanted to stop this cruel, savage ordeal, but I was the foreigner, the outsider. All I could do was sit and watch. Realizing I was not breathing, I let out a sigh.

"Start the test," the imam told Ali.

Slowly Ali looked down into the basket. As he did, the cobra's head reared up above the basket rim. It was a big king cobra with a beautiful pattern on the back of its hood that contrasted with its lighter body color.

Ali got down on his knees and placed his face about

eighteen inches away, face-to-face with the shiny black snake eyes. At any moment it could easily strike.

Again the crowd was pleased and whispered its approval.

Mustafa was jubilant. "No other boy has ever done that. Most boys slowly wave a stick to charm the snake. Then they try to touch it. That is all the test requires."

As we watched, Ali remained motionless, staring at the snake. The crowd was silent. Ali's hands hung limply at his sides. Several minutes went by. The big snake swayed from side to side, its black tongue darting in and out almost faster than the eye could see.

Very slowly Ali began moving closer to the weaving head. He stopped with his head no more than a foot away from its deadly fangs.

Every eye was on him. The imam was slowly turning his head from side to side as if to say, "No, that's too much. Just try to touch it."

The snake stopped swaying and stood like a dark statue. Ali chose the moment and slowly leaned forward until he was an inch from the cobra's face. He stopped there, frozen. Then, with a slow and deliberate movement, Ali bent over and kissed the snake on top of its head.

The watching crowd nearly went crazy. Mustafa was so excited he pounded my back in enthusiasm.

Ali sat back, slowly stood up, and smiled at the imam.

The people cheered until they were hoarse. The men shouted and stomped their feet.

Mustafa was shaking hands all around. "The seeress was right. Ali is going to be a leader like no other before him," called the proud father.

The imam raised his hands and called for quiet. It took several minutes for the jubilation to die down.

"The last test is for strength," he announced. "Let it begin!"

Three men each carried a large boulder onto the platform and let it drop with a thud. The smallest weighed perhaps fifty pounds; the second, some seventy-five; and the third, about a hundred.

Mustafa explained the test to me: "Ali must move each stone from where it sits to where the imam stands. These stones weigh about the same as goats and our largest sheep. To be a man, one must be able to lift a sheep in his arms and carry it from danger."

"Let the test of strength begin!"

The imam walked across the platform and placed his staff on the floor. Ali, about twenty feet away, walked over to the first boulder. He squatted down and grasped it. With a grunt he managed to lift it clear off the floor, carry it, and lay it at the imam's feet.

"And now the second stone!" the old man ordered.

"Little Ali will not be able to lift that stone," Faud said in a louder than necessary voice to his brother Abdul, sitting beside him. "I have seen him try that before. He will fail."

Everyone in the audience, including Ali, heard the comment.

With all eyes on him, Ali squatted by the second stone. He wrapped his arms around it, struggled to stand up, and failed.

A moan rose from the onlookers. They all were hoping that the young, brave Ali would succeed.

"I think this is too much for my son," Mustafa confided to me in a whisper. "He is brave, but he is just a boy whose muscles have still to grow."

Ali grunted and tried again. He struggled, and his knees shook, but he lifted the stone. With sweat running down his face, he took ten faltering steps, then placed it next to the smaller one at the imam's feet.

The audience cheered loudly.

Just one more stone and the tests will be over, but the last stone, I thought, was one even a strong man would have trouble lifting.

"Let's see the little hero move this one," challenged Faud.

"Continue the test!" called the imam.

Ali squatted by the stone and tried to get his arms far enough around it to try a lift. Ali was probably as strong as most fourteen-year-old village boys, but his arms were too short.

The imam saw the problem, but the tests, once started, had to be completed. A hush fell over the audience as Ali struggled again to grasp the big stone. He could not get a hold. He was going to fail.

"Mighty imam," I interrupted, "it is not Ali's strength that is lacking; it's his short arms. I have a suggestion to make this test fair."

The Arabs all stopped chattering and looked at me. I was interfering with a traditional ceremony, but I could not stand by and watch Ali fail when he had done so well.

The imam glared at me with reddened eyes. "What do you suggest, man of faraway lands?"

I got up and walked over to the platform near Ali. I unbuckled my heavy leather belt and handed it to him. I motioned for him to bend over and whispered some advice in his ear.

I returned to my seat, and Ali said to the imam, "I am ready to try the third stone."

The imam looked at the belt and then at the stone. "Start the test!" he said.

Ali squatted next to the stone and slipped my belt around

it. He looped each end of the belt around his hands and dragged the stone close against his body. With the belt placed like a sling around the stone's lower girth, he leaned back slightly with legs spread and, with a loud grunt, attempted to raise it.

The stone moved only slightly. Placing his feet even wider apart, Ali pulled the belt tighter and leaned back on his heels. This time he slowly managed to stand, lifting the stone from the ground.

A low cheer arose from the onlookers. With the stone held tightly against his body, Ali walked painstakingly across the platform to the imam. The holy man looked at him in wonder, then raised his hands to signify that the test was successful.

But Ali did not put the stone down. Instead, he turned and slowly made his way back across the platform until he was just above his father and brothers seated next to it. He smiled at his father, then loosened the belt, letting the stone fall with a crash at Faud's feet.

"Dear brother," he said with a grin, "I dropped the stone. Will you hand it back to me?"

Faud knew his bluff had been called.

A huge cheer arose from the crowd. This time even the women were on their feet shouting.

The imam walked over to Ali, bent down, and kissed his left cheek, then his right cheek. "Ali, son of Mustafa, of the house of Zambir, you are from this day forth a man. Let no man doubt that you have passed the tests."

Every man, woman, and child in the village cheered. Ali's mother hurried to his side and hugged him close. "My son, my heart aches for your pain, but you have made me the proudest mother in the world."

The rest of the day was spent in celebration and in eating

the feast prepared for the event. By late afternoon everyone was tired and ready for a long rest.

I explained to Mustafa that I had to return to America for a while but I would be back in a few weeks. I bade my Arabian friends good-bye, gathered up my backpack, and started back toward the wall for the long climb to the rim.

Ali walked with me and shook my hand in farewell. I climbed up about a hundred feet and stopped to look down at him. "It has been a wonderful visit. I will come again in a few weeks, Ali, after I return from my trip to America."

"Go with Allah's blessing, Mr. Wayne."

12

The Magnificent Eagle

ON MY RETURN to Saudi Arabia I was anxious to travel to the great canyon to see how Ali and his father were coming along with the baby eagle, Samson, but a last-minute change in my company's schedule required me to be posted across the Arabian Peninsula near the Persian Gulf. I was told my assignment there would be for six weeks, but it lasted seven long, hot months.

It was early January before I was finally posted back to the high western desert at Khamis Mushayt.

After checking in and working for six straight days, I finally got a two-day weekend off. I happily cranked up my old Rover and headed for the great canyon.

The rainy season was in the middle of its one-month duration. I was amazed and delighted to see what a little water could do to the high, barren desert. There were patches of green everywhere.

The thorn trees had tiny clusters of bright green leaves between each two-inch spike. I saw numerous camels nibbling from the trees, their tough lips parting the thorns to get to the juicy new growth.

The desert was like a different world after a rain. I saw many small animals frolicking on the cool plateau as I drove along, happily singing an old John Denver song, "Sunshine on My Shoulder."

Stopping near the rim of the canyon above the village, I was surprised to see two men working the winch I had left there more than seven months ago. I got out, and as I approached them, I recognized Mustafa and his eldest son, Faud. They were slowly winding the rope down to the valley floor below. I looked over the wall and saw a large bundle wrapped in a cloth, slowly going down.

"Allah's greeting," I called to my old friend.

Mustafa looked up and saw me and told Faud to keep lowering the rope. A look of happy surprise lit Mustafa's face as he got up and embraced me and kissed me on both cheeks.

"Wayne, it is good to see you. Where have you been for so long? We thought you had left forever, and Ali was very sad."

"I have been working on the other side of Saudi Arabia, in Dhahran, all these months. I just returned this week. I am very anxious to hear about the baby eagle."

As I finished my sentence, I was aware of Faud's hate-filled eyes watching me. He made no attempt to greet me or even speak.

"Wayne, there has been much trouble between Faud and Ali. It has caused me much loss of sleep."

Faud locked the winch and stood up. He had grown taller while I was gone and looked stronger. In his waistband he wore a long, curved knife. His hand tightly gripped the handle as he spoke. "I have seen the city of Khamis Mushayt, and I have seen other white faces there. I do not like you Americans. You should go back to America." There was a cold, angry edge to his voice.

"Faud, you bring shame upon me!" shouted Mustafa. "Mr. Wayne is my friend. I demand an immediate apology." Faud was silent and stared into his father's eyes. Then he said, "I am the eldest son, and it is I who should be the village chief. You are too old and weak to rule. I say the American should never visit us again."

Mustafa was shocked and hurt at Faud's words.

Faud was insanely jealous of his father's feelings for Ali and held me partially responsible. He felt that as the first-born he should be the favored son.

"Faud, leave at once and do not come back until you can obey your father."

Faud stood with clenched fists and looked as if he were going to strike his father, but he finally backed off. Angrily he turned from the canyon wall and ran away across the plateau.

"Please forgive my son, Wayne. He has never been so disobedient before. A few days ago he and Ali got into a fight. Ali was badly beaten but refused to tell me what they had been fighting about. Since Faud has visited the world above our village in the big canyon, all he can talk about is changing the way we live."

Mustafa explained how he and Ali had rigged up the winch to lower things to the village.

"We have a great surprise for you. The eagle has grown strong and has been in training for several months. He was just at the right age when you caught him. He is doing things none of our other birds has ever done. Come, let us go down, and I will show you."

We climbed down the crevice route and picked up the bundle when we reached the bottom. I was amazed to see it held canned food and even more surprised to see clothing.

As we neared the village, Mustafa shouted, "Ali, Mr. Wayne has returned."

What I saw next was beyond my imagination. Little Ali, who had grown taller, emerged from around the corner of a house and stood in the street, waiting for us. On his left shoulder was the biggest bird I had ever seen.

A large leather cover was draped over Ali's shoulder on which the eagle sat, its talons lightly holding on.

"Is that Samson?" I asked incredulously.

"Yes, Wayne. This eagle has become Ali's pet. He has grown so strong he can pick up a small goat and fly away with it. So far he has taken several goats and sheep while training to catch wild animals, but he is learning."

Ali stayed back and did not attempt to come near me. "Mr. Wayne! Oh, Mr. Wayne, it is so good to see you again! Excuse me for not embracing you, but Samson is very dangerous to anyone else. Only when I put him on his stand and tie him down can I get close to anyone."

Samson was beautiful. He was a full-grown Arabian golden eagle with a mixture of light brown, black, and white feathers. The sunlight gave him a golden shine that made him look almost like polished brass.

"Mustafa, this is the most magnificent bird I have ever seen."

"He is truly a gift from Allah," replied Mustafa. "Ali, put Samson up so we can share tea with Mr. Wayne and tell him what we have done with your big pet."

As Ali started to walk away, the eagle kept his black eyes on me. He had a large head with a black turned-down beak that ended in a knife-sharp point. His talons were at least three inches long, each one sharp as an ice pick. I could hardly believe what I was seeing.

Ali was walking around with one of the world's fiercest predators on his shoulder as if it were a huge parrot. I just stood and watched in awe as they walked toward the aviary building.

Mustafa and I went to his house, where his wives were busy with their chores. "Mr. Wayne and I will have tea," he ordered softly. The oldest woman gracefully left the room to start the tea water on the ember pit she kept burning day and night.

"We have worked very hard the past few months to train Ali's eagle. It was very difficult at first, but with patience, we have managed to get good results.

"This eagle is not like the falcons and hawks we hunt with. They hunt for the bloodlust of it and return to us only because we feed them well and care for their needs. With Samson, it is different, very different. Ali stayed with his bird day and night for two months. He fed him, talked to him, and let him become used to him. Ali would let no one else come near Samson.

"That is one of the reasons Faud became so angry. The whole village has been watching and talking about Ali as he trains his bird. Faud wants to be admired, too, but Ali is the one people praise.

"After five months we took the bird with us to sit on Ali's arm and watch the other birds train and hunt. The first time we released Samson to see if he would grab the meat on the training line, he broke loose and flew away. I must tell you, Ali was heartbroken, and so was I.

"There were six of us hunting that day, and all the birds were gone when Samson got away. One by one the birds came back with their prey. As night approached, the others went back to the village, but Ali and I waited.

"He kept whistling the call he had taught his bird to return to. We had never used it with Samson in free flight, so we did not know if it would work. Finally, at last light, we had to go back.

"As we walked along, nearly home, suddenly we heard a rustle of feathers and a shrill eagle call. Samson was heading right for us, dropping his feet for a landing. Ali quickly held up his arm, but Samson went on by.

"Ali whistled again, and Samson whistled back, then wheeled in flight and dived straight to Ali's waiting arm and landed, almost knocking Ali to the ground. My son was so happy he danced and shouted.

"The most remarkable thing about Samson is that he will let Ali stroke his head with his hand. None of the other birds will let their masters do that without biting their fingers."

As Mustafa finished telling me about what I had missed, Ali came in and joined us. We talked for a long time, and Mustafa smoked his hookah pipe, using a mixture of dried seeds for tobacco.

A cold wind was whistling through the house, causing all of us to pull our clothes tight. On nights in January in the high Arabian desert temperatures fall below freezing, and the only source of light and heat in the room was the fire and two oil lamps that burned animal fat in woolen wicks.

I asked Mustafa what Faud would do up on the top, alone in the cold night.

"Faud is a man and must live as one. He will be safe," he said sadly.

I was again given my old bed in the large hay-filled loft. Within minutes I was snuggled into the deep woolen blankets, trying to get my feet warm. The last thing I remember that night was the sound of the wind moaning through the canyon.

I awoke to the soft nuzzling of a young goat as it licked

my face. I looked up into two goat eyes looking back down at me.

"Hello, Mr. Goat," I said, reaching up to stroke his bearded face.

"Baaaaa."

Because it was very cold, I dreaded getting out of the blankets. Just as I was hastily pulling on my boots, Mustafa appeared at the stairway. "Good morning, Wayne. It is a fine cold day to see the birds hunt. Come, we will have breakfast."

I was pleasantly surprised to see Faud seated with his brothers.

"Faud has something he wants to say to you, Wayne," Mustafa said as he gestured for me to sit down beside him.

"Yes, Mr. Wayne, I want to apologize to you. I spent the night on the rim thinking about my life and the future. My father and I had a talk early this morning. He has raised me to be the next chief of this village, and I realize now that more than anything I want my father to be proud of me. He has forgiven me, Mr. Wayne. I hope you, also, will accept my apology."

"Yes, of course, Faud. Someday you will become a village chief your family will be proud of."

When we finished a hearty Arabian meal of bread, hand-ground from grains, vegetables with rice, and hot tea, Ali asked, "Can we show Mr. Wayne how Samson can hunt today?"

"That is exactly what I have planned, Ali, as soon as you and your brothers finish your chores. Today is a good day to test Samson's skills."

Mustafa led the way as most of the village men followed him to a high, rocky ledge overlooking a great sweeping valley.

It was a procession to remember. Twelve men carried their

falcons or hawks on their arms, each followed by his own cheering section. In all, there were about seventy-five men and boys assembled on the high overlook.

Mustafa had Kitcha on his left arm. The female peregrine falcon had a beautiful leather hood, trimmed with gold beads on which the light danced in the bright afternoon sun.

But most imposing of all was Ali, with Samson seated on his left shoulder. With each step Ali took, Samson balanced himself anew, sometimes flapping his huge wings to keep from falling off.

Samson had a strong woven leather sleeve on each leg. Each sleeve had a steel ring attached to it, and both rings had heavy leather straps that held the big bird so it could not fly before it was freed.

This was to be Samson's first official hunt with the other birds. He was anxious to fly, and the other birds were restless in his presence.

As the last of the falconers calmed their birds and settled down on the overlook, Mustafa stood at the rear of the group with his sleek hunter poised on his leather-wrapped left arm. Next to him stood Ali with Samson nearly weighing him down.

Ali's mother had used three thicknesses of leather to make Ali's vest, adding extra-heavy wool padding on the left shoulder. On his arm was a matching padded leather cover for the launching and recovery of Samson.

It was exhilarating for me to stand there, with the cool wind blowing down the canyon, and listening to the rustle of the bird's feathers. There was a great deal of laughter and joking among the hunters and the spectators as they shared stories of past hunts. Faud had come along, too, which pleased Mustafa. He was happy to have all his sons there.

"The wind is coming from the canyon, so the birds have

an excellent day for the hunt," Mustafa said before he raised his right arm and announced: *"Let the hunt begin!"*

The falconers separated from the others and began their routines for freeing the birds.

The men gave the birds fresh meat, which was ravenously gobbled down. One of the larger red hawks struggled fiercely to get free, anxious to be in the air. Its owner spoke soothingly trying to keep it calm until its turn came.

Mustafa called for the men, one by one, to release their birds. Both the birds and the men were excited as the leg restraints were unhooked. As each bird was freed, it flew directly into the wind blowing up from the canyon.

The falcons and hawks flew out across the huge drop-off that fell away to the canyon floor a half mile below. I watched the birds as they separated to look for quarry. It was beautiful to see the noble birds flying to the hunt as their kind had done for thousands of years.

Mustafa let Kitcha go. The big falcon flapped her strong wings and dropped down into the valley.

Finally it was Ali's turn to set Samson free.

"Ali, you must trust Samson to return. He will sense it if you have any doubt, and fly to his freedom. You must keep your thoughts with him and think as one. Do you understand?"

"Yes, Father, I am ready."

Mustafa explained to me that Arab men had a mental bond with their birds. They believed this connection was stronger than the leather thongs that held the birds. It was a mysterious process, one that only a few Arabian falconers ever mastered. He said that he had not mentioned this during the first hunt I attended because I would not have understood.

Ali closed his eyes and stood motionless for a full minute.

Surprisingly, Samson, who had been anxiously flapping his big wings, was still, too. It was as if boy and bird were locked in a mental exchange.

Ali unsnapped one of Samson's legs, then the other. The eagle let out a shrill whistle and flew away. A cheer from the group showed its pleasure at the eagle's launch.

Samson did not fly down into the valley like the other hunters. He flew higher and higher until he was just a speck in the sky. Silently I hoped the eagle had not said his last good-bye, to fly away forever.

I wondered if Mustafa and Ali were thinking the same thing. We looked at one another and then back at the speck that had all but disappeared in the distance.

"Father, Samson has not flown so high before. What if he does not return?"

"My son, be one with your bird. See what he sees, feel what he feels. Become Samson, Ali. You can do it."

Ali closed his eyes and stood motionless. Then a slight smile spread across his face. He looked serene and happy. There was definitely something happening here that had no explanation in science.

"This, Wayne, is what I tried to tell you about how we control our birds. Ali is here, yet he is with his eagle, high above the canyon, floating free on the warm air that lifts him to the heavens. No man can explain how this happens. The falconers who cannot master this mental unity never achieve great success with their birds. It is not written about in any book; it cannot be taught. It is between man and bird and comes only after total trust has been established."

Mustafa had a faraway look in his eyes as he spoke. I could see he, too, was mentally with his bird, sweeping down the valley in search of prey. I looked at the other falconers.

Each one stood silent now, some staring into space, others with their eyes closed.

I wondered if it was really possible for a man to communicate with the mind of a bird or an animal. I had known instances where people seemed to be able to communicate with dolphins, but that was under controlled circumstances where the mammals quickly learned what the humans wanted by watching their body language or hearing their vocal intonations.

This was totally different. I was not ready to accept this mysterious form of man-bird link that Mustafa believed in. I knew there must be a logical explanation . . . but what was it?

Thirty minutes passed. Two falcons had returned with rabbits. Another thirty minutes passed. Then the other birds started returning, one by one, each carrying a small animal or a game bird in its talons. As each bird dropped its prey, its master called out to it with praise, holding his left arm up for a landing.

The birds seemed ready to be back with man, and each unerringly found its master's arm. It was breathtaking to see the birds return from their freedom. Each was beautiful in its own way. The three hawks among the falcons were larger and landed a bit harder than their lighter cousins.

The next to return was a falcon that carried a ratlike animal with reddish fur. I had no idea what it was.

Kitcha was the last falcon to return. She had a large, fat rabbit, still struggling as it was dropped at Mustafa's feet.

With the men happily chattering and comparing catches, Ali remained silent. He was looking into the sky, still smiling. "He's returning now, Father," said Ali.

"Very well, my son."

Was it possible that Ali really knew where his eagle was?

I chided myself for being so inflexible that I could not believe something just because it did not meet my own set of rules.

"He is not alone." Ali said it matter-of-factly.

The group of men stopped talking and listened.

"Samson brings a female with him."

A murmur arose from the assembled villagers. One was pointing behind the plateau where the canyon wall rose to the top of the great chasm about a mile from where we stood. I squinted to see better. It seemed impossible to me that Ali could know this.

There, high in the sky, were two large birds, wings motionless, floating gently downward. They glided side by side, wingtips nearly touching. Lower and lower they came, still not flapping their wings. They looked like two airplanes with their landing gears down, coming in for a landing.

About a quarter of a mile away one of the birds started flapping its wings and rose rapidly above the other. The second bird started flapping, too, and caught up with the first. Both flew directly over our group about three hundred feet high.

"It is Samson, Father!" shouted Ali. "It is Samson."

"It is indeed, and he seems to have a friend with him."

I was awestruck. It was Samson. He was easy to identify because of his size and colors. Ali had told us Samson was not alone, and now the big eagle was overhead with a second eagle. My logical mind did not want to accept how Ali could have known.

Ali whistled his long, shrill birdcall as the two flew overhead. Then Samson wheeled and dived with wings tucked. He hurtled like a falling rock, straight at the assembled crowd. I wondered how he could pick his owner out of all the men wearing white robes below him, but by now I was ready to believe anything was possible.

Samson spread his wings and slowed his descent but flew right over Ali, just above his head. He then quickly climbed to join the other eagle still circling above us. The two flew lazily in a large circle, again wingtip to wingtip.

"My son, it looks as if Samson has found a female. He wants to return to you, but he wants to be with her, too. He is torn between his link with you since he was a baby and his new feeling of freedom to be with other eagles. If he does not come back, then it is as Allah wishes it."

Ali watched in silence for a while. Then he whistled again and again.

Both eagles flew lower, heading toward us. It was a magnificent sight: two strong, beautiful birds of prey, flying down into a large group of people whom they should naturally fear.

"Ali, hold up your arm. The rest of you, get back," ordered Mustafa.

Ali did as instructed. The two eagles came straight at Ali. A few feet away Samson fluttered his wings for a landing while the female stayed at his side.

Samson hit Ali with such impact that he lost his balance and stumbled, almost falling. With a wild flapping of wings, Samson settled down on his leather perch on Ali's shoulder. The female flew low overhead, calling her eagle cry. Samson looked up to her from his perch on Ali's shoulder and shrilly whistled back.

"Ali, snap on the leg harness!"

"No, Father, if Samson wants to leave me, he is free to choose."

I had never seen Ali disobey his father before, but Mustafa nodded his approval.

The female flew higher and away toward the canyon wall. "Samson, you were supposed to be hunting animals to eat, not lady friends." Ali laughed. "Well, you came back. That is the important thing now."

The sun was already behind the canyon wall, casting a shadow across the valley as we returned. Everyone was happily chattering about the hunt while we walked back to the village. I had to go back to my job for another week, but I would go refreshed by what I had witnessed today.

Mustafa assured me that Ali and Samson would continue training during the week. He wondered if the eagle could learn not to devour prey once he had caught it. Time would tell.

I said my good-byes to everyone and started my climb out of the canyon.

13

Ali and the Prince

AFTER I GOT BACK to work, I could not stop thinking about Ali and his handling of Samson. I kept remembering his faraway look as he mentally became one with the eagle.

In the course of my work for the aircraft company, I often had to deal with members of the Saudi royal family. I had an appointment that week to discuss some military business with one of the king's sons, Prince Faisal. He was a pilot in the Royal Saudi Air Force, and I had often flown with him across the empty stretches of his barren country.

It was during our long flights that I had learned of his love of falconry. He told me many of the royal princes had falcons and often entered them in the contests held around the Arab world and elsewhere. It turned out that Faisal was one of the most renowned falconers in the world. I was anxious to tell him about Ali and his eagle.

I never knew exactly when or how Faisal would arrive. When he drove up in a bright red Mercedes-Benz convertible, I was surprised to see a white falcon perched on his shoulder.

The prince wore a beautiful white tobe, a flowing robe, enhanced with gold piping. On his head was a jewel-studded double headband to hold his ghutra, or headdress, on.

"Hiya, there, Tex," he called out to me from his car.

"Hiya, Prince! How you doing?" I called back.

"Jump in and we're outta here." He laughed. He enjoyed using American slang. He always amazed me with his command of the English language. He spoke it with only a trace of the guttural accent many Arabs have. He had gone to Harvard and MIT.

I got into the Mercedes and slid down into the leather seat. The falcon on Faisal's shoulder jumped a bit as I got in but soon ignored me.

"My brother Sultan and I are competing in a contest and I thought you might like to come along."

"What about the business we planned, Prince?"

"We can discuss business as we drive along, my American friend. You know the old saying 'All work and no play . . .'"

Faisal sped the Mercedes up to 130 miles per hour as we raced across the nearly abandoned road that led toward the city of Abha, about 30 miles distant.

The Saudi desert is much like Arizona with sparse, low bushes, lots of rocky hills, and a few thorn trees. Every few miles we passed a camel caravan plodding down the road. Faisal always slowed down and waved to the wandering Bedouins as we passed. He was a royal prince and perhaps would one day be king, but he never forgot his roots.

By the time we got to Abha, my voice was hoarse from shouting above the wind, but we had settled our business so now we could relax and enjoy the rest of the day.

It seemed a good time to tell Faisal about Ali and Samson. Faisal's reaction was surprise when I told him about my experiences in the village.

"I have heard about the people of the rift valleys who are renowned falconers," he said. "To have a hunting eagle is a dream I, too, have had, but I know of no one in Arabia who has been able to train a young eagle to hunt, and now you tell me that a young boy has done so. I must see this boy with his eagle. Will you take me to him?"

I assured him that I would, but I wondered how the village people would react to having a royal prince visit them.

The falcon hunting contest in Abha was a far cry from what I had witnessed in the village with Mustafa and Ali. It consisted of perhaps fifty Arabs assembled with expensive cars and trucks. Each had an array of cages and fancy equipment. Dressed in the standard white garb of summer, the men looked wealthy beyond belief. They wore diamond rings, Rolex watches, and designer sunglasses, and they drove expensive cars.

As I looked at these oil-rich Arabs with their fine cars and equipment, I thought of the men of the village with their simple handmade cages and perches. What a contrast!

The wealthy Arabs also had a different style in working their birds. Each contestant held his falcon while a pigeon was released about fifty yards away. As the pigeon was released, the contestant freed his falcon. A timer and three judges, who were scattered across the hunting area, monitored how long it took the falcon to reach its prey and how it attacked.

Most of the falcons flew toward the pigeon and attacked after gaining altitude and swooping down for the kill. The pigeons often averted the falcons by changing direction, climbing, or diving.

Many times the hunters overshot their prey. After a set time limit was signaled, the falconer blew his whistle, calling his bird to return to him.

The judges ruled on style, speed, and attack maneuvers and awarded three prizes.

When Faisal's falcon was released, it flew at an angle toward the direction the pigeon was heading. By cutting the prey off with a closing side attack, the falcon could save time. If a falcon first had to fly behind the pigeon and then catch up, it lost time.

Most falcons or hawks used the catch-up attack because the pigeon could not see it approach from behind.

As Faisal's falcon headed for the pigeon, it looked as if it were going to catch it on the first pass, but just as the hunter tried to grab the prey, the pigeon darted down and to the left, causing the falcon to overshoot.

Turning, trying to catch the speedy quarry, the falcon flew upward, then dived toward the frightened bird. Again the pigeon quickly turned and flew at a right angle to the falcon's flight path and caused it once more to overshoot.

Faisal had had enough. He knew the time was too long, so he blew his whistle for the falcon's return. Like a boomerang, the falcon gave up the hunt and flew straight back to land on the prince's outstretched arm. I saw the pride in Faisal's eyes as he petted his bird.

"That is enough for today, my little friend," the prince said fondly to his bird.

After the meet we drove back across the high desert and talked about falcon training and what an art it was. I explained how the villagers trained their birds, using hand gestures, whistles, and what I could only refer to as thought transference.

"I have heard of these men who seem to control their birds with their minds," Faisal said. "It is an art that goes back thousands of years to ancient Persia. I thought it was all an old fairy tale, but perhaps there are men who can still do it. Will you take me to meet these people? I will bring a helicopter, and we can fly into the valley tomorrow."

I knew the noise and sight of a big helicopter would frighten both the villagers and their animals, so I carefully considered my answer.

"I'll take you to meet Mustafa and Ali under two conditions: One, I go down alone first and ask permission to bring you; two, we use no helicopter. We must climb down."

Faisal looked troubled. "I haven't done much mountain climbing"—he sighed—"but okay, I'll give it a try. There's a first time for everything."

"No problem, Prince. You'll do fine. How about next Thursday?"

Thursday and Friday, not Saturday and Sunday, are the weekend days in Arabia.

"Yes. We'll go see this eagle boy on Thursday."

I drove the Rover faster than necessary across the high, flat plateau, stirring up great clouds of dust and scattering herds of wild burros. Prince Faisal and I were having great fun as we maneuvered around large rocks and gullies on the way to the big canyon where Ali lived.

It was a bright and clear morning with just a nip in the cool air here at ninety-eight hundred feet above sea level. When we reached the rim where the long line ran down the cliff, we got out, and I pointed out Ali's village far down in the valley. The morning sun had not yet risen high enough to light the shadow falling across the entire valley, but the distant western ridges were aglow with crimson.

"We'll use the power winch on the Rover to lower us down into the valley. I'll go first and call you on the radio when I find out what the plan is. Then you can wind me up with the winch, and I'll lower you down and follow with my rappel gear. When we come back, I'll climb the crevice and power winch you back up."

I hooked myself into the harness, stepped to the rim, and was over, with Faisal lowering me steadily. I was on the valley floor in twenty minutes.

I called Faisal on the radio as I walked toward the village. "Okay, Prince, I'm on my way. Be ready to join me soon."

"Okay, Tex."

The outlying villagers waved to me as I passed, calling out greetings. Mustafa, Ali, and his brothers were working on a rock wall in front of their house when I arrived. Faud and Abdul were among them.

They all stopped when I walked up. "Praise Allah, Wayne is back," said Mustafa.

"I have missed you, Wayne," Ali said. It was the first time he had not called me "Mister."

"I have missed you as well," I answered.

"Boys, it is time for a tea break. Hamad, ask your mother to prepare it."

Ali's brother hurried off as ordered. We went to the house and drank the hot tea prepared for us. I explained there was a visitor above who wanted to come to the village to join us.

"And who is this visitor?" asked Mustafa suspiciously.

"His Royal Highness Prince Faisal, son of King Khalid."

Mustafa's eyes opened wide. "The royal prince wants to visit this lowly village?"

"Yes, but I wanted to ask your permission before I brought him."

"He is welcome!" exclaimed Mustafa. "But why would His Majesty want to come here?"

"Prince Faisal wants to see Ali's eagle."

Ali was stunned. "To see Samson?"

"Yes, Ali. And to meet you all."

"Tell the prince we will kill a sheep for a feast. He is most welcome."

Mustafa called his wives and told them to prepare for a feast.

I thanked my host for the tea and headed for the door. "I'll be back with the prince within an hour."

The word spread like wildfire. Within minutes the whole village was buzzing with excitement. I made my way to the wall, hooked up my body harness to the rope, and keyed the walkie-talkie. "Okay, Prince, bring me up."

My walkie-talkie hissed and sputtered, "One lift, coming right up."

The rope tightened, and I was on my way. By now I was so used to the cliff face that I knew nearly every hand- and foothold along the route. Within twenty minutes I was on the rim with Faisal.

I explained the rappel process to him, hooked him up to the body harness, and over he went. I lowered him down slowly. Concerned about his comfort and safety, I stopped him about every fifty feet to talk to him on the walkie-talkie. He assured me he had piloted jet airplanes most of his adult life and had no fear of heights.

When he was down, I suggested he unhook and stand back, so I could rappel down, using hand brakes. Leap after leap, I dropped to the valley floor. Faisal helped me store the harnesses before we started for the village.

The first young shepherd we saw dropped to the ground in a royal bow when he realized a royal prince was in the valley. Faisal stopped in front of him and said it was not necessary to bow, but the boy never moved.

As we entered the village, everyone we saw dropped to the ground. Faisal waved and bade them rise, but few did until we passed.

At Mustafa's house a handwoven rug was lying at the stairway entrance. Mustafa, in the doorway, bowed to the ground. After the prince bade him stand up, I introduced Faisal first to Mustafa and then to the sons, and Mustafa invited us into the dining area. The wives peeked from behind a split bamboo screen that divided the kitchen from the eating room.

"I have heard that you have some of the finest hunting birds in all Arabia," Prince Faisal said to Mustafa. "I would very much like to see them. And Ali, Wayne tells me you have a trained golden eagle."

Ali blushed and lowered his eyes.

"Your Highness, I will order a special hunt in your honor," said Mustafa. "I think you will never see another hunter like Samson, Ali's eagle. Allah has smiled on us. The eagle is the mightiest hunter ever to be trained in our valleys."

"I look forward to it," Faisal said, smiling.

We left the house and introduced the prince to the whole village. Mustafa chose three men to bring their falcons and participate in the hunt.

In the aviary he hooked up his prize falcon, Kitcha, to his left arm, then led the way, with Ali close behind, to Samson, who was separated from the other birds.

"This is Samson," said Ali proudly.

Samson, with his beautiful golden brown feathers, massive beak and talons, stood on the oversize perch with wings raised partway as if he were about to take flight.

"Ali, I have never seen such a magnificent bird in all my life," exclaimed the excited prince. "Is it possible you have tamed him?"

Ali pulled himself up to his tallest and said, "Samson can fly faster and higher than any falcon. He is master of the air."

The villagers fell in behind us as we took the five birds to the high ground hunting area. Samson, perched on Ali's shoulder, was excited. His bright eyes kept blinking rapidly, and he fluttered his big wings, eager to fly.

Once at the area the villagers sat quietly on the ground while the prince, Mustafa, Ali, the three other hunters, and I stood ready for the start.

"Today we will hunt for other birds," Mustafa said. "When we see a bird appear, I will order a hunter to release his falcon for the chase."

There were many birds in this part of the valley, from sparrows to hawks, as well as other falcons and wild eagles on the hunt. There were several Egyptian vultures flying high overhead, their white undersides marking them clearly.

"Salman, release your bird," Mustafa ordered the first hunter.

Salman loosened the tie, dropped his arm, and the bird was away. It flew strongly and straight toward a flock of three mid-size birds crossing the canyon from our left.

I watched the prince as Salman stood transfixed. The villager did not move but stared straight at the flock in the distance. His falcon flew like a released arrow and caught the flock from above. There was a flurry of falling feathers as the falcon sank its talons into an unsuspecting bird.

Salman smiled as his bird wheeled and came back to the assembled villagers. When it was close, Salman whistled, and the falcon flew to him, dropped the partridge, and landed on his arm.

"How did the bird know the quarry?" asked the prince incredulously.

Salman gave a thin smile and said, "A man and bird must work as a team. The bird knows what I want from it."

Twice more Mustafa ordered the hunters to send their birds off in pursuit of their quarry. Twice more they returned within five minutes, having achieved success.

I could see Faisal was enjoying himself. He was witnessing what few outsiders had ever seen, men and birds somehow working together in an unseen bond.

"Now Ali and I will release Kitcha and Samson for the flock you see there coming down the valley." Mustafa raised his arm. "Ready?"

Ali unhooked Samson's tether and held him by his right leg.

"Now!"

Kitcha flew from Mustafa's arm. Samson opened his huge wings and climbed rapidly away from Ali.

Both Mustafa and Ali stood like statues, their eyes on the distant flock.

At first the speedy Kitcha was leading, but soon, as he achieved full speed, Samson passed her. The eagle looked as if he were flying at a leisurely pace, except that he passed the falcon at half again her speed.

As we all watched, Samson flew above the flock, then dived into their midst. Kitcha was still en route when Samson made his kill and started back.

Faisal watched Ali carefully, trying to see what he was doing to control his eagle. He could see nothing. Samson came in fast and, swooping over Ali's head, dropped the bird.

He turned and flew straight back, passing Kitcha, returning with her bird, and caught the flock before it was half-way across the canyon. Again he struck with lightning speed and knocked a bird from the flock. The birds scattered in every direction, but Samson, with a bird already in his talons, struck for a third time.

As we watched, the big eagle flew toward us, laboring in flight. When he got near, we could see what was slowing him down. The villagers stood and cheered as they, too, saw what had happened. Samson had a large bird in his talons and another clamped in his beak.

He went straight to Ali and dropped the bird from his talons. He held on to the one in his beak and landed on Ali's shoulder.

"Good boy, Samson! Good boy!" Ali stroked his bird with his right hand and said, "The other bird is yours."

Ali pointed his arm and finger toward an open stretch of grass. Samson lifted off and flew to it. As we watched, the eagle ripped the bird to pieces with its beak and ate the entire thing.

"It is awesome! It is incredible beyond belief." Faisal was lost for words. "This Samson is like no other bird that has ever been trained. I must bring Ali and his bird to show my father. Mustafa, may I have permission to take Ali to visit the king?"

"As Allah wills it, Your Highness. My son has my permission to go."

"What about it, Ali?" I asked. "Would you like to go to see the king of Arabia?"

"Oh, yes. Yes! Yes! Yes!"

"Then it is settled," said Faisal. "I will show you and your eagle to the world. In one month my father is hosting a falconry contest at the Abha palace. The best falconers in the world will be there. I would like you and Samson to compete."

Ali was overwhelmed with joy.

After we got back to the village, a great feast was held in honor of the prince. There was much eating, much talking, and much laughter. By late afternoon we had full stomachs and full hearts.

Since it was getting late, the prince and I had to start back so he could be at the air base to fly the next morning.

☐   ☐   ☐

On a quiet afternoon three weeks later, just as I arrived home from work, I heard a helicopter thumping nearby. I went outside and recognized the Royal Saudi Air Force insignia on its side.

It slowly lowered and landed on a large rocky area near our water well. The dust it threw up created a small pair of dust devils that danced across the barren landscape and died out. The engine whined down, and the door opened. It was Faisal.

I walked over to the chopper and greeted him. "Great entrance, Prince." I laughed.

"I want to fly into the valley and get Ali and the eagle. I sent two men to the valley yesterday to get his father's permission. He and the eagle will be ready and waiting. I will land there. I also have many gifts for the village in the chopper. Can you come along?"

As it turned out, I could.

Faisal piloted the helicopter, and we lifted off, scattering a herd of wandering sheep grazing nearby. As we flew away, I saw the shepherd shaking his fist at us for frightening his animals.

The distance that took me an hour to drive by Land Rover took about five minutes by air.

"Here we go," said Faisal as he started a steep descent into the canyon. My stomach tickled as the big jet chopper dropped like a rock. With deft control movements, he maneuvered the helicopter like a fluttering butterfly.

On a rock-lined terrace below, I saw Mustafa, Ali, Abdul, and several others, waving. As we landed, their eyes were wide with fright at the sight of the aircraft and the noise.

Faisal shut the engines down, and we got out. Ali, his

father, and his brothers were standing by a large split bamboo cage. Inside, Samson flapped his wings madly.

The prince greeted Mustafa like a friend, kissing him on both cheeks. He shook hands with Ali and his three brothers and, turning to the eagle in the cage, said: "Well, Mr. Samson, today you will fly high without wings. But soon you will fly for Ali in the most important falconry contest in all of the Arab states."

The prince asked them to follow us to the helicopter with the cage. When we got close, the boys all slowed down. Mustafa reassured his sons that the machine was part of the "upper world" and nothing to be feared.

I helped unload several boxes of supplies the prince had brought for the village. They contained food, medicine, bolts of material, tools, boxes of matches, candy, cakes, and fruit.

Mustafa was stunned. "Our village owes you a great debt, Your Highness. May Allah bless you and your children for centuries to come."

"I have ordered the government to bring you more supplies, and there will be a doctor sent to examine all your people. Since your village is so remote, getting a road up to it from the sea to the west cannot be done immediately, but we will look into some way to provide supplies to your village."

Mustafa was overwhelmed. So were his sons. I wondered silently about what was happening. This village that had lived virtually unchanged for thousands of years was about to be hurtled into the twentieth century. And a fourteen-year-old boy from one of the most remote spots in Arabia was being catapulted into the modern world . . . all because of an eagle.

14
Ali's Royal Welcome

"THAT'S MY FATHER'S western palace," said Faisal, pointing out a large building on the edge of the great Arabian escarpment. "Look over that way, Ali. See that city on the slope of the mountains? That's Abha, where we will land."

Ali, nose pressed to window, was looking down from the helicopter at the country of which he was a citizen yet about which he knew so little. I couldn't imagine what he was feeling. I could only compare it with how I might feel if I were suddenly thrown into the future by some magic time machine.

"Mr. Wayne, I'm glad you are with me."

"I'm glad, too, Ali. I know you and Samson will enjoy your royal stay."

Faisal called the control tower at Abha, asked for landing instructions, and within ten minutes we were on the ground in front of a large hangar with Arabian flags flying in the brisk wind. As we got out of the helicopter, a Rolls-Royce limousine was waiting. The driver saluted Faisal and held the door for us to get in.

We sped away toward the palace outside Abha, about a

twenty-minute drive. Behind us, in an enclosed air-conditioned Mercedes-Benz truck, Samson, with his own driver, followed.

Faisal kept pointing out areas of interest to Ali. As we approached the royal palace grounds, the huge gates swung open, and we drove inside. It was like something out of a storybook.

The palace had a tall minaret on each corner. A massive shining central tower mirrored the sun. It was breathtaking. Along each side of the entrance were long pools surrounded by deep green grass and flowering shrubs that seemed out of place in the desert.

The limousine stopped in front of a large ornate wooden door that must have been fifteen feet tall. Four Saudi soldiers snapped to attention as Faisal stepped from the car.

"Welcome to our home, Ali, Wayne. Come, let me show you to your rooms."

Ali was speechless. He stared at each new thing he saw in the cavernous palace. The richness and grandeur were beyond imagination, but Ali seemed more taken with the paintings that adorned the walls. Many were of former kings of Arabia, and one caught his attention.

It was of King Faisal, son of King Saud, seated on some large cushions. A large gyrfalcon was perched on a round stand next to him.

"Who is the man with the falcon?" asked Ali.

"That is my grandfather King Faisal. He is dead, but he loved his birds and was a great hunter."

"How does one get to be king?" Ali asked in all seriousness.

Faisal looked at me, held his hands palms upward, and seemed lost for an answer.

"You must be the eldest son of the king," I said. "And when the king dies, you will become king."

"I think I would one day like to be a king," Ali said.

Faisal burst out laughing and patted Ali on the back. "Little friend of the birds, you can be a king sooner than you think. You can become king of the falconers if you and Samson win the contest."

"Where is Samson being kept?" asked Ali.

"Come along, I'll show you." Faisal led us across the highly polished marble floors to an inner courtyard where two men were just setting down Samson's cage. The bird was screaming at them and trying to bite their fingers through the slats.

In the courtyard were six round falcon stands, carved from olive wood and padded with gold-studded leather. On each was a white falcon, the most prized bird of all royal falconers.

Faisal had told me the birds were nearly priceless, the result of a breeding program that often produced multicolored birds instead of the rare white ones. These falcon's feathers were white, tipped with black, making the birds look almost regal themselves.

Ali drew in his breath with a noticeable sound. He had never seen white falcons before. "These birds are more beautiful than I can say. My father should see them. . . . He would not believe me if I told him."

"Your Samson is the most beautiful bird I have ever seen, Ali," replied the prince. "I know he is young and does not have the training to compete with many of the birds that will be in the contest, but it is good experience for you both to compete. These falcons are the finest in all the world. They have been trained by the best falconers and are going to be entered in the contest by my brother and me. We have hopes of beating the emir of Kuwait, who has taken the championship for the past three years."

Ali looked the prince right in the eyes and, with all seriousness, said, "My Samson can win against all other birds. He will be the champion."

Faisal started to laugh but did not want to hurt Ali's feelings. He knew the rules and requirements would tax the finest teams on the contest field.

"You will have every chance to do that, Ali. I promise you. Now, why don't you feed and care for Samson? I'll have fresh meat brought to you. That big T perch is for Samson. He needs to get used to his new home, so be sure you tie him securely."

As Ali opened the cage door, the two men who had carried it to the palace stepped back in fear.

Reaching inside, Ali spoke softly to his eagle. "I know you miss your home in the village, Samson, but we will be here for only a short time. Are you hungry?"

He reached in and gently stroked the big bird's head, running his hand down between the tucked wings. Samson pushed his massive head against Ali's hand as he enjoyed the petting.

After a few minutes of this closeness Ali took the leather straps and snapped them onto the ring on each of Samson's legs. He then put on his leather arm cover and stuck his arm under the bird's chest. Samson stepped up and onto his arm, nearly flattening it to the cage bottom with his weight.

In one swift movement Ali had the big bird out and perched on the stand. After he had fastened the straps, Ali stepped back. "There, now you have some freedom."

The nearby falcons all began to flap excitedly on their perches. The eagle was easily three times their size. Samson raised his huge wings as if to fly and held them open. He gave a shrill eagle whistle that excited the falcons even more.

"It looks as if Samson has taken charge of the roost," said Faisal.

Ali fed Samson meat that was delivered on a gold tray brought by a servant. The big bird ate ravenously, then settled down to preen his feathers.

"Now it is our turn to eat and talk of the contest."

Faisal led us to an ornate dining room, where there was an early lunch waiting.

After we had eaten, Faisal asked a servant to show us to our rooms. I knew I had better go with Ali at first because he would not know how to use the toilet or sink.

His room was large with a massive bed on a raised pedestal. The stained glass windows cast a mixture of shimmering colors on the white marble, floor, creating a rainbow effect.

"This is the toilet," I explained. "After you have finished, you push this, and the water will clean the bowl."

Ali looked in wonder at the water standing in the carved onyx bowl. I then showed him the sink and water taps. Each tap was made of gold in the shape of a dolphin. I turned the hot water on, and water poured from the dolphin's mouth. Ali drew a sharp breath.

"How can it be that water comes from this thing?" he asked in amazement.

He stuck his hand in and felt the water, drew it back and smelled it, then did it again. He tried the taps himself, laughing each time water spilled out.

After I had shown him the shower and explained how to bathe in it, he said, "It is all so confusing. Water from a fish. A machine that flies like a bird. Walls that make rainbows. I cannot seem to keep all this in my head."

"Don't worry, you'll soon get used to these new things.

I'll come for you in an hour. Faisal told me he would have some new clothes sent up for you."

As I left Ali, I knew he was going to examine everything in the room. It would be great fun for him.

The king was due to arrive tomorrow to open the falconry contest. He would bring with him the emir of Kuwait. It was going to be a big three days.

After showering and changing clothes, I went down to find the prince. He was sitting on a leather couch in one of the luxurious living rooms, talking to another, younger prince named Turki. I had no difficulty remembering that name. Turki was about eighteen, one of the younger princes, and he spoke English with a noticeably cultured accent.

After we had talked for about an hour, I excused myself and went up to get Ali. I hardly recognized him. Two servants had helped him dress in a beautiful new tobe of white silk and a red checked ghutra, with a golden agal, a woven rope that held the headdress in place. On his feet were new leather sandals trimmed with handcrafted designs and gold-colored piping.

Letting out a long whistle, I bowed from the waist. "Is this Prince Ali of the eagles?" I asked.

"I feel a bit foolish wearing these clothes, but the material feels good on my skin. I wish my father could see me now; he would be very proud," Ali said.

"Mustafa is proud of you, Ali, whatever you wear. He is a lucky man to have a son like you."

Then Ali did something I had never seen him do before. His eyes filled with tears as he thought about his father back in the canyon.

"Come, my fancy friend," I said. "We have much to see and do before tomorrow, and there is another prince who wants to meet you."

We went downstairs to join the two royal princes. Both stood to greet us. After Faisal had introduced Prince Turki, we all went to show him Ali's eagle. Like others who saw Samson for the first time, Turki was struck by the bird's size and beauty.

"May I touch him?" Turki started to reach toward Samson, but Ali quickly jumped between them.

"Samson will let no one but me get near him. He has bitten and scratched several who have tried. I'm sorry, but he is dangerous."

Turki smiled and stepped back. "You are a very lucky boy to have such a bird. I should like to buy him from you. Name your price."

"Samson and I are a pair," Ali replied. "Where I go, he goes. Where he goes, I go. I could never part with him."

"See, Turki, I told you," Faisal said. "You cannot buy everything."

The four of us took Samson out to the field where the contest was to be held. Ali carried the big bird on his shoulder. Samson was excited and kept flapping his wings, rising as far as the restraints would permit.

Ali fed him some meat he had carried along and then let him fly free. The big eagle soared high overhead as if inspecting the new terrain. He climbed higher and higher until he was just a speck in the blue sky.

Then Ali stood perfectly still and closed his eyes. We watched as Samson turned and dived toward the ground, hurtling at an ever-faster speed. The speck grew larger and larger, and Samson came back to his master, drawn by an unseen, unheard command. With a fluttering of his mighty wings, Samson landed on Ali's shoulder.

Ali pointed to the sky, and Samson immediately was airborne again. For three hours we watched enthralled as the boy of the canyon put his eagle through his paces. Turki and Faisal were nearly speechless with awe and envy. They both had thought the white Arctic gyrfalcons they would use in the contest were more skillful hunters than any large bird, but now, as they watched Ali and Samson, they felt a flicker of uncertainty.

We returned to the palace as the sun was sinking behind the mountains of Asir to the west. It had been a long, exciting day for us, and after dinner Ali and I went to bed early, both of us anxious for tomorrow and the first day of the contest.

15

The Contest

ALI AND I were up at 6:00 A.M., while the night was still black as velvet, to prepare Samson for the contest. The stars were twinkling as we made our way to the contest field with Samson flapping on Ali's shoulder.

On the horizon the star cluster known as the Southern Cross blazed with an intensity that made us stop and stare at it. I knew ancient seamen had used it to steer their sailing ships by. I explained to Ali how it marked the south while the north star, Polaris, marked the north. But he already knew both celestial bodies as well as others used by Bedouins for centuries as they wandered the trackless deserts.

Standing on the palace grounds, surrounded by ragged mountains, we watched the first rays of dawn. The desert was a beautiful place at sunrise.

We were not alone. We could see dozens of expensive campers and trucks with license plates from almost every neighboring Arab state parked on the road leading to the contest area. The contestants and their birds had arrived overnight.

There was to be a hawk class with goshawks and Cooper's

hawks that hunted ground prey. There was an open hunting class, where the gyrfalcons and peregrine and Egyptian black falcons were to hung winged prey. The winners of each class would then compete for the grand prize. They would be timed to see how long it took them to reach a specific flying target, make the capture, and return to their masters' arms. The judges would be watching the handler's technique, the bird's speed and attack style, and how well it responded to its master's control calls.

We hurried to let Samson get the sight and scent of all the people. He needed privacy before the field was filled with noise and the sky with birds.

We walked down the sloping grassy field for about a quarter mile with Samson watching every step intently. He wanted to be free to fly, but Ali had him securely fastened to his leg restraints. A covey of grouse suddenly took wing with a whirring noise that made Samson strain to get into the air. He was hungry and wanted to hunt. We continued around the perimeter of the main contest field, examining every foot.

"I want to let Samson fly free for a short while before we go back for breakfast. I am going to release him here."

Ali reached up and unsnapped first one leg and then the other. Samson sat still, although freed. Ali raised his right arm and pointed skyward, and Samson immediately flew off. It was a new trick for them both, and I was impressed.

"Watch this, Wayne."

Ali placed his hand on his shoulder and stood still. Samson, still gaining altitude, wheeled in flight and dived straight back and landed on Ali's shoulder.

"Wow," I said in English. "Very impressive, Ali. Any more tricks?"

Again he pointed, and Samson flew. He then swung his arm and pointed westward. Samson turned in flight and flew in a westward direction. They repeated the trick to the east and to the north.

We walked to the palace gate, and Ali stopped and placed his hand on his shoulder. I could barely see Samson in the distance, but evidently the expression *eagle eye* was well founded because he came at once and landed.

It was the closest control of a wild creature that I had ever seen. I knew that his father and ancestors had done it before him. Now it was Ali's turn.

We headed back to the palace, secured Samson to his stand, and had breakfast. I could see Faisal was ready. Gone was the tobe, replaced by Western dress. He wore a beautiful leather jacket with matching riding trousers tucked into shiny knee-high boots. He was all business and set to win.

By the time we returned to the contest area, there were hundreds of people gathered. A large grandstand with comfortable leather sofas on colorful oriental carpets, stood in the middle of the high platform. The flag of Saudi Arabia flew from a hundred different masts, lining both sides of the field. The contest was to begin at 10:00 A.M., and by 9:30 everyone was in place. The stands were full, the contestants were ready, and all were anxiously waiting for the king to arrive to start the show.

Ten tall black men from the Sudan, each with the typical cheek scars from their rites of passage into manhood, stood ready to sound the long trumpets they held across their chests. They wore red jackets trimmed with gold buttons and black riding pants tucked into high boots. The air was filled with expectancy and excitement. The judges were at their assigned places in the field. The quarry release men were ready with their cages of birds and animals.

At five minutes before ten o'clock, the trumpeters lifted their golden horns and sounded the royal salute. The king's motorcade was coming. Ten black Mercedes-Benz cars rolled along in perfect formation. From both front fenders of the lead car flew the king's royal flag.

The cars stopped by the platform, and the drivers got out. Each car door was opened at the exact same moment. The king emerged from his car and looked over the vast group of people, animals, and birds, then climbed the stairs, followed by his entourage of sons and brothers. He gestured to the trumpeters. Another blast from their horns, and there was silence.

The king raised both arms high. He looked out over the crowd, turned his head from side to side, and shouted for all to hear, *"Let the contest begin!"*

The chief judge announced the order of events, stated the rules, and called for the first five contestants to get ready.

The morning events were for the ground hunters. These hunters' birds went after small animals on the ground and were trained to ignore other birds in the air. Most of the entrants were from Libya and Egypt with a few from Morocco and Algeria.

When the judge gave the "start" order, a man downfield released a small hare from a cage and fired a pistol with a blank cartridge. The contestant released his bird at the sound of the shot, and the hunt was on. Each bird flew down the field, looking for the movement of game. Once the game was spotted, the bird would dive on the animal, sink its talons into its back, and lift it off the ground. The bird had to carry the hare back to its master, drop it, and land on his glove. The timing started with the shot and ended when the bird landed on the glove. The judges then marked their ballots and waited for the next contestant.

For three hours each contestant did his best to show style, ability, and bird control. In the end a Moroccan businessman won first place. A hawker from Egypt came in second, and a Libyan's red hawk was third. There were a hundred dead rabbits that were carefully gathered up to become part of the feast that followed the contest.

Before the aerial hunters' contest began, tea and lunch were served to everyone, picnic style. The king left for the palace and then returned to open the second half of the contest.

There would be one winner in three separate categories. Then each winner would perform a demonstration, and one would be selected as grand prize winner.

After the king was seated, the chief judge announced: "The free-flight hunters category is now open. Each contestant will be judged in each of the three categories. The first will be the handler's ability to direct his bird to the proper quarry. Two grouse will be let go, one from each side of the field. I will announce which quarry your bird is to hunt after the opening shot has been fired. The second category will be judged on the basis of the time it takes the hunter to get to the quarry, make the capture, and return. The third category depends on how the handler and his bird respond to my commands. The three handlers who earn the most points will then compete for the championship. The winner will receive one million Saudi riyals from the king." That was approximately $300,000 in U.S. currency.

The first entrant was from Libya. His black falcon flew off his arm, left the field, and was not seen again.

The second contestant was an Arabian royal family member with a female peregrine falcon. As his falcon started downfield, the judge called, "Left target!" To direct his bird to the correct grouse, the falconer blew two short blasts on a gold whistle. The falcon darted left and caught up with the grouse before it crossed the field limit mark. It hit the grouse hard, captured it, and flew back to its master. But instead of landing immediately, it flew twice in a big circle before it dropped the prey and landed on the disappointed handler's glove.

For three hours we watched the dozens of contestants try their skill.

When it was Faisal's turn, he selected his favorite white gyrfalcon, took its ornate hood off, and stood ready.

Bang! The signal shot was fired. His bird flew off his arm straight as an arrow downfield.

The judge called, "Right target," and Faisal immediately blew three short blasts on his control whistle. The gyrfalcon veered right, caught the grouse from the rear with its talons, and turned to fly directly back to Faisal. It dropped the quarry at the prince's feet and landed smoothly on his arm.

A great murmur went up from the crowd as they recognized the best performance of any bird so far.

Faisal smiled. He knew he was way ahead on points. His style on both launch and recovery was nothing short of perfection.

Prince Turki was next. He also used one of the royal gyrfalcons. At the shot his bird's launch was a little slow. It was up to the handler to anticipate the gun and drop his arm the moment it sounded. Unfortunately Turki's bird failed to go to the right target, got the wrong bird, and was disqualified.

Three more royal princes using gyrfalcons did their best. Two were so close to Faisal's time that none of us knew who was ahead.

"Uh-oh, here's the man to beat," whispered Faisal as the emir of Kuwait took his place on the mark. "He has the finest birds in the world and uses the best trainers. He beats us nearly every year, but I think I have a chance if he isn't perfect this time."

Ali watched the emir intently, all the while stroking Samson's feathers as he stood next to the big bird's stand.

"They say the emir's birds are the fastest in the world, Ali. They train every day, so don't feel bad if Samson can't beat them. You can always come back next year."

Ali looked up into my eyes and said seriously, "Samson and I have some surprises for all of you."

Bang! The emir's black falcon few rapidly from his arm, staying low over the ground. "Right target," called the judge.

A single high-pitched whistle sharply sounded. The falcon stayed low but turned to intercept the grouse crossing from the right release point. Within seconds the hunter was on the prey, making the capture. It swooped down, caught the grouse, and flew low back to the emir. By staying low, the falcon cut the time needed to get to the target. It saved valuable seconds by not flying up against gravity and then having to dive for the kill.

A loud cheer went up as the spectators voiced their pleasure with the black falcon's performance. Faisal groaned, "He's done it again. Look at the judge's smile. It's all over."

Several more contestants sent their birds downfield, but everyone knew the emir of Kuwait had won again.

Finally the last contestant was called. "For the first time in the history of this event, we have an entrant with an eagle. . . ."

The crowd's response was so loud it drowned out the announcer.

"Please . . . please . . . quiet!"

The noise died down but did not stop.

"From the village of Ezratu in the great rift valley to the west, Ali, son of Mustafa, will demonstrate the hunting skills of his golden eagle. This is Ali's first event, and his eagle has never flown under these rules before."

Laughter rolled across the field as men who had attended hundreds of falcon contests looked unbelievingly while Ali stepped up to the starting mark. He stood quietly as Samson opened and closed his wings in excitement.

Bang!

Samson was airborne before the sound of the shot faded away. He flapped his big wings and gained about a hundred feet in altitude as he went straight downfield.

The grouse handlers on each side of the field threw up the target birds, but suddenly a second grouse appeared on the right. A cage had been left ajar, and the second bird flew with the first. The right target had two grouse flitting at full speed across the field toward a grove of trees.

The judge did not see the double release until it was too late. He ordered, "Right target!"

A moan went up from those who saw the mistake. Ali saw it, too, but he instantly pointed his arm right.

I heard a man nearby say, "Look, the boy does not use a whistle. Instead, he uses his arm to control the bird."

Samson veered toward the right but not toward the grouse. At first it looked as if he had not sighted the target. Unlike most hunting birds that go after a prey's actual position in the air, Samson was lining up his attack point out ahead of the target, where it would be when they met in the air.

He was twice as high as the falcons had hunted, and true to his eagle heritage, he dived on his prey, using his superior speed to catch them.

Everyone on the field saw the speed with which the eagle closed the gap to the two grouse. Tucking his wings close, he hurtled down at the fleeing pair. They were about fifty feet apart when the trailing one was caught in Samson's talons.

He never missed a beat with his mighty wings and quickly

came up behind the second quarry. He grabbed it from flight, holding it in his other foot.

Ali saw what Samson did and opened his arms wide, palms facing each other, and quickly clapped his hands. Samson noticeably sped up, boring a hole in the sky, directly back to Ali.

Ali held his right arm straight out to his side, then dropped it. That was his signal for Samson to drop the prey. As Ali's hand stopped at his side, the two grouse were already dropping at his feet.

Samson was moving so fast he had to flare his wings widely to stop on Ali's shoulder, nearly covering him from view.

A roar went up from the crowd as hundreds of people registered their awe for a performance the likes of which they had never before seen.

In the royal grandstand the king stood up and motioned for everyone to stand. The applause was deafening. It went on for a full five minutes until the king stepped down from the platform and walked over to Ali, still standing on the start mark.

"Ali, never in my life have I seen such a performance. Your eagle has shown us what a mighty bird can do in the right trainer's hands. You make me proud to be your king."

Samson was flapping his wings, anxious to hunt more as Ali stood face-to-face with his king.

The chief judge walked over with his stopwatch in hand. He said to the king, "It's impossible. This boy and his eagle have shortened the record by a full ten seconds, and the bird caught two quarry."

The king made the official announcement. "Ali, son of Mustafa, from the house of Zambir, I declare you the winner in all three categories. The emir of Kuwait places second, and Prince Faisal places third."

A roar went up in the crowd. "More, more, more!" the people shouted. They remained standing, every person straining to see the small boy with his eagle.

Ali pointed skyward, and Samson flew off. The rush of air from his wings stirred the king's robes.

As the eagle climbed, Ali pointed left, and Samson flew left. Ali pointed his arm straight up, and Samson climbed rapidly until he was nothing more than a speck in the sky. Then Ali turned his back to the field and faced the king directly. "What would you have him do, my king?"

The king thought for a moment and then said, "Have him fly to the right and come down lower."

Ali closed his eyes and stood in silence.

The king looked puzzled. "Did you hear me, Ali?"

Ali remained still.

What happened then made the king cover his mouth with his hand in disbelief. He squinted and looked high in the sky at the eagle. Samson was hurtling earthward, turning to the right as he dropped.

"Allah, be praised!" mumbled the king. "I have heard of this ability from old books about the Bedouins, but now I am seeing it with my own eyes."

Ali, still with his back to Samson, said quietly, "Now Samson will fly low over the crowd and come to me."

We all watched with wonder. Samson flew down close to the ground, circled just above the heads of the cheering crowd, and came toward us.

Faisal was speechless. He looked first at Ali, then at Samson approaching. The king stepped back to watch.

Samson slowed to almost a stop and fluttered to a light

landing on Ali's shoulder. He stood there with wings open to cool himself.

"Now, with your permission, I would like to have ten target birds released at once," Ali said to the nearly speechless judge.

The judge so ordered. Down the field, from both left and right, ten birds were released, flitting in every direction.

Ali stroked Samson's head a moment and then pointed to the flying grouse. Samson lifted off, again rustling the tobes of those nearby. He flew high and fast toward a group of three grouse close together.

The eagle quickly caught up with the birds and dived on them from above. For a moment we couldn't see what was happening. Then, one by one, the grouse fell to the ground, mortally wounded by Samson's beak and talons.

Wheeling sharply in flight, Samson went after two more grouse near the center of the field. He flew right up behind them and knocked them from the air. One dropped, but one tried to get away. Samson flew above the fleeing grouse, sank his talons into its back, and it, too, fell, mortally wounded. The crowd cheered wildly.

The other grouse were near a grove of trees off to the west side of the field. Each was trying to get away the best it could. Ali turned, pointed his left arm toward the fleeing grouse, and Samson rapidly closed the distance to the nearest one.

With a flurry of feathers, he caught one, then another, knocking them to the ground. The three remaining birds made it to the protection of the trees.

Ali turned again with his back to Samson and closed his eyes. Samson turned, flew higher, and started back toward us. As he neared, Ali pointed his arm straight up. Samson's big wings bit the air as he climbed higher and higher.

"Say the word, my king, and Samson will come to me."

The king watched as Samson continued flying higher and higher. "Now, Ali."

Ali touched his left shoulder and held his hand there.

Samson started back down. He looked like a falling rock with his wings tucked up close. About fifty feet up he opened his wings and fluttered down to land on Ali's shoulder.

The spectators went crazy. There was shouting and cheering as they all tried to get close to Ali. The king's bodyguards had to act fast to restrain them.

The king went back to the platform and motioned to the governor of the city of Abha to join him while Ali secured Samson to his perch. "Ali bin Mustafa, from the village of Ezratu," announced the governor, "come up to the platform!"

Now that the contest was over, Ali was nervous and hesitated.

I whispered to him, "This is your moment. Go to the king."

He walked to the stairs and went up. The governor praised him loudly and quoted from the Koran about boys growing into men with dignity.

The king stood while all became silent and watched as he reached down and kissed Ali on each cheek. Keeping his hands on Ali's shoulders, he said for all to hear, "Ali, you make me proud to be an Arabian. I will tell your father and your whole village of my pride in you. My son Prince Faisal has told me of the needs of your village, and I am ordering a special team to go there and report back to me how I can help your people."

The king presented Ali with a check for one million riyals and then kissed him again.

Ali beamed with pride and joy.

The festivities continued well into the night. There was

feasting, music, and folk dancing. The king's kitchen staff had gathered up all the birds and animals slain in the hunt and prepared them as part of the feast held in honor of the winner of the contest.

Ali was the happiest boy in the whole world that night. Everyone wanted to meet him and ask questions about how he controlled his eagle. He was polite to them all, but his answer was always the same. "You must become one with the bird."

We all had witnessed a closeness between a wild creature and a human that defied explanation.

16

Ali Flies with Samson

THE NEXT MORNING Faisal, Ali, and I loaded the helicopter with Samson's cage and several boxes of food and supplies for the people of Ali's village.

I tried to explain to him how much money he had won, but he had never had any money and could not understand what it meant. "With this piece of paper you can buy anything you want for yourself or your family. You can even buy your father a plow so he and your brothers would not have to work so hard. You can buy tools and clothing . . . anything."

"But we already have everything we need," replied Ali sincerely.

Faisal, listening to our conversation, smiled at me and rolled his eyes. "How many people can say that?" he asked.

I sat back and waited for the chopper to lift off. The prince gave both Ali and me a helmet with a radio headset so we could talk over the roar of the engines as we flew along.

"Here we go." Faisal gave the engines fuel, and we lifted off in nose-down position, slowly climbing toward a mountain pass to the south of Abha.

"Ali," I asked, "how would you like to fly like Samson, high and free?"

"Wayne, people cannot fly like the birds except in machines like this. Why do you joke with me?"

"I am not joking, Ali. In America where I come from, we have something called a hang glider that will carry a man into the sky. It is made of metal and a material called nylon. It is simple to use, and once you have mastered it, you can fly like a bird. On my last trip home I brought my glider back with the idea of using it on the slopes by the compound. I've been so busy coming here on my days off that I have not had a chance to use it. Each time I stand on the canyon rim and feel the warm wind blowing up the cliff face, I think about gliding out over the canyon gorge. I've flown it in similar places but none quite so high and steep as your canyon."

"Whoa there, Wayne," interrupted Faisal. "Those things can be dangerous. They don't have an engine, and the only way you can go is down."

"Not exactly correct, Prince," I said. "By using warm air thermals, a hang glider can actually climb and stay aloft for a long time. In fact, the present world record for distance traveled is about ninety-five miles. If we use the warm air updrafts from the canyon for lift, I figure I can get a long, tall ride."

Ali was listening intently. Even though he did not know the technical words we used, he was following our conversation carefully.

"Can I really fly with this—" Ali tried to say the word in English.

"Hang glider," I coached. "It is called a hang glider, Ali, because you hang in it and glide through the air."

Prince Faisal still wasn't convinced. "Suppose you get a good lift and fly like a bird for a while, then land down in the canyon depths. How do you propose to get the glider back to the cliff top after you land it?"

"I've thought about that, too. Here's how I see it. If the thermals are strong enough, we can gain altitude and get well above the canyon rim, circle over the gorge until we lose the updraft, then head back toward the cliff to catch it for another lift. If we want to land in the rift valley, there are several dry, sandy riverbeds to land on. Then all I have to do is pick it up and take it back to my rope pulley. The glider only weighs about fifty pounds, so hoisting it back will be easy."

"My friend"—Faisal sighed—"Americans always amaze me. They never admit some things can't be done and are usually right. Who would have thought men could walk on the moon?"

The flight to the village lasted only twenty minutes. When the villagers saw us coming, they ran to the landing pad to greet us. As soon as the blades stopped whirling, Mustafa and his family were at the door. I swung it open, and everyone shouted at once.

"Father, Samson won. He won the contest!"

"Can this be? Praise Allah! Praise Allah!"

All of Ali's brothers and sisters, including Faud, crowded around to hear the news. "Ah, my little brother has returned as a hero," said Faud, smiling. "Congratulations! We are all proud of you." Mustafa, pleased that his oldest and youngest sons were once again on good terms, embraced them both.

Ali's mother, completely covered in her black chador, reached out her arms to her son and hugged him and kissed his face, making him blush. For once Mustafa did not tell her to restrain her feelings in public.

Faisal explained to Mustafa and the assembled crowd what Ali and Samson had done, adding, "I have never before seen the king so excited about anything. He has vowed to help your village and make each of your lives better."

After thirty minutes of questions and answers Faisal and I had to leave. I had to be back at work, and Faisal was due to fly his F–18 Hornet in an aerial display the next day. We said our good-byes, and I closed the helicopter door.

The last thing I saw as I looked down was the line of villagers headed back to their homes. In the middle I could see two men carrying Samson's cage.

Over the intercom Faisal voiced his feelings. "I'm a royal prince, one of the wealthiest men in the world, and have everything. Yet little Ali from his remote village has so much more. The relationship he has with that eagle cannot be bought."

For the next three weeks I was busy at the airport, finally saving up enough time to take three days.

I had worked on my hang glider until it was perfect. I made a few dry runs down some fairly steep slopes near the compound and found it working perfectly. Several of my American friends tried it, too, and for a few days I was the hit of the party, taking many for rides.

I knew the big two-man glider was safe when handled by someone who knew how to fly it, and I was determined to take it to the canyon the next day for the ultimate test. I rolled it up and tied it to the Rover, then went to bed for a good night's sleep.

By early morning I was on my way to the canyon. At the rim I stored my equipment and climbed down the crevice route, now as familiar as an escalator to me. I found Ali tending the sheep and goats. He waved and called as I walked up.

"Are we going to fly like an eagle today?" he asked.

"Yes, today is the day. I'm going to practice. Then, when all is ready, you are going to fly with me."

Ali's eyes went wide. "Oh, Wayne, I must run and tell my

father and brothers. They will want to watch me fly like a bird."

I followed as he ran down the dusty path, calling, "Father! Father! I am going to fly like Samson!"

When I asked Mustafa's permission to take Ali for a ride in the glider, he scratched his beard and paused a long time before answering. "Wayne, I trust my son's life to you. I do not believe man can fly like a bird, but Allah is great, and anything is possible."

As Ali and I left to climb up to the rim, I noticed things I had not seen in the village before. There were pipes running from a spring up higher, carrying water to several terraces under cultivation. There was a gasoline-driven generator humming by the village well.

Four men, wearing uniforms of the Saudi Energy Department, with a lightning bolt emblem across the back, were constructing a metal building.

When I asked one of the men what he was building, he told me the king had ordered an electric generator to be built. He also told me a road was planned from Ash Shuqayq, on the Red Sea, to the village.

"It will take more than a year, but when it is finished, this village will have access to the Red Sea, so the people can trade their produce," he added proudly.

The king had been true to his promise. Progress was coming fast to change life in this quiet village forever.

We hiked back to the canyon wall and made the climb back to the rim. Assembling the glider was easy, but I took special precautions to ensure that the braces were screwed in just right and that the guy wires were so taut I could strum them like a guitar string.

It was a big glider, with red, white, and blue nylon panels. "It looks like a flying American flag," I explained to Ali.

Getting it to the cliff face was tricky. The plateau breeze kept lifting one side, then the other, nearly jerking it from our hands. To do this right, we needed a launching platform, but for now, I knew as soon as I stepped off the cliff, the nylon would drink in enough air to float me easily away from the jagged wall of the canyon.

I snapped myself into the harness, got a good grip on the control bar, and said, "This is it, Ali! I'll see you back here in a few minutes if all goes well."

Ali just grinned as I took a deep breath, ran a few steps, and jumped off into space. Almost immediately I was lifted by the air moving up the canyon wall. I leaned right, and the big kite moved off to the right. As soon as I cleared the cliff face, I placed my body and feet into the nylon sling. Now I was like a giant butterfly, sailing on the wind.

The cool wind of the plateau gave way to the warm thermal air boiling up from the hot rocks and soil of the canyon floor. I experimented with technique. I banked left, then right, and flew straight ahead again.

"Wow!"

It *was* like being a bird. The glider was steadily going down toward the canyon floor, but I found I could turn back toward the cliff and catch an updraft and rise back above the rim.

Ali shouted encouragement and waved his arms from the rim each time I soared his way. For fifteen minutes I flew the glider, then turned back over the plateau and landed about a hundred feet behind the edge.

Ali ran over and excitedly said, "That looks wonderful, Wayne. Can I fly like a bird now?"

"Soon, Ali, but I want to try it again first, to be sure it is perfect."

We carried the glider back to the edge, where I inspected

it and found it airworthy. Then Ali watched as I ran a few steps and soared out over the chasm. Again the warm air lifted me gently.

Off to my right I saw two eagles gliding on a thermal. They lazily circled upward, not moving a muscle. I leaned right to dump some air from my left wing and drifted toward them. They saw me and flapped their wings to move away.

Suddenly I felt a rush of very warm air. I was in the thermal. Up, up I went. Within seconds I was a thousand feet above the canyon rim and going up fast. I could judge the thermal current by the temperature of the air around me, so I kept banking back toward the plateau until I felt the cool air. As soon as the glider was in the cooler air, I began to lose altitude. It was easy to glide back over the rim and land again.

"Ali, it will be getting dark soon. I want the conditions to be perfect before I take you for a ride, so why don't we camp here for the night and take our big flight tomorrow when the sun is high in the sky?"

"Oh, yes, Wayne. I am very hungry. Did you bring some food?"

"Of course, Ali. Help me stow the glider and set up our camp, and we'll make a delicious meal on the camp stove."

Ali and I cooked dinner, ate, and talked until the cold night air drove us into our sleeping bags.

It was well into daylight when I heard, "Hey, wake up, Wayne. It's morning."

"Good morning, Ali."

"Good morning, Wayne. Are we going to fly soon?"

"We are indeed," I answered. "Would you like to help me cook breakfast first?"

"Yes, I like to help you cook. In my home my mother and the women always do the cooking. I didn't know men knew how."

The day began to warm as the sun rose higher. The weather was perfect, with a slight breeze blowing. I gave Ali some more scrambled eggs, which he gulped down. "By noon, Ali, the thermals will be warm enough to fly."

I intended to repeat yesterday's flight paths, using thermals to climb above the plateau level and then glide back to it when I wanted to land. By noon everything looked perfect. "Okay, Ali, it's time to fly like a eagle."

I expected him to be apprehensive, but he did not seem to be the least bit afraid. I strapped Ali in first and then myself and explained, "We will hold the glider level and run, just as I did yesterday, then jump off the cliff."

Ali never hesitated.

"Okay, here we go," I said in English as we started to run. The cliff face suddenly dropped away under our feet. We were airborne.

"We are flying! We are flying!" shouted Ali.

I adjusted my weight and slipped into the nylon sling and had Ali get into his. With his extra weight, the glider started dropping faster than when flown solo.

I turned back toward the cliff, caught the updraft, and up we went. After climbing about a thousand feet above the rim level, I turned, and we flew out over the canyon, almost directly over the village. The only sound was the soft rustle of the nylon glider fabric as the air moved past it.

Ali was captivated as I explained about the warm air's rising and how to control the glider's direction. He looked out over the canyon, where several eagles were floating on the warm thermals. "Look, there are eagles, and we are flying just like them."

Higher and higher we flew, as the warm air supported us. Ali was in his sling next to me, and we both hung there over the great canyon and watched the world go by. The bird's-eye view was beyond description. The canyon swept for fifty miles in front of us, intersected by dozens of side canyons, joining to create the great escarpment of western Arabia.

Far below us the villagers were gathered in the street, calling up to us as we sailed silently overhead.

"Everyone looks so tiny, like ants," Ali said. "Hello, Father . . ." he shouted down.

Many voices echoed up to us from the canyon depths, but one stood out. It was Mustafa's.

"Allah be praised! Ali! . . . Wayne! . . . You are flying like the birds."

I looked over to Ali and saw a broad smile on his face as he looked down toward his village, trying to pick out his father. "Father, release Samson! Let him fly free," he called down. He shouted it twice more.

Then all the voices stilled beneath us. We heard Mustafa call back. "Samson will be set free. . . ."

We had lost the thermal and turned back toward the cliff for an updraft lift before landing. We glided over the rim and landed smoothly.

I wondered why Ali had asked for Samson to be released. He answered my question before it was asked. "Can we fly again? I want to fly side by side with Samson. I know he will come if I call to him."

"Okay, Ali, this time we'll fly farther out over the canyon and use the same thermals the birds over there are using," I said, pointing to several hawks circling nearly motionless on an invisible platform.

"If we get that far away, can we make it back to the rim to land?" asked Ali.

"We're going to land in the valley on a wadi this time," I answered. "That way we can get a long ride and pass low over the village."

We checked everything, hooked ourselves into the glider, ran to the rim, and were off again. When we reached the thermal, we went up and passed right through the floating birds, scattering them in every direction. Higher and higher we soared.

I noticed Ali's eyes were closed, his body still. It was how he had looked when he performed with Samson for the king. When I thought we were high enough for a broad, sweeping flight down across the valley to pass low over the village, I leaned left and dumped enough air to start us away from the thermal.

The only sound was the wind rustling the glider's nylon. We were still too high to hear the villagers. Suddenly we heard another sound. I recognized it immediately. It was wind over feathers.

"Look, it's Samson," shouted Ali.

Sure enough the big eagle was right beside us, sailing on outstretched wings, flapping them occasionally to adjust his glide to ours.

Then we saw a second eagle. It was Samson's friend. She was gliding down to join him.

It was a fairyland, Disney World, the last day of school, and the circus all at once. We were flying free in one of the most beautiful spots on Planet Earth, Ali, Samson, his female companion, and I, swooping out across the great chasm. Side by side in the glider, followed by the eagles, we descended into the canyon over Ali's village.

Ali called down, "It is Ali . . . Ali . . . Ali. . . . I am flying! I am flying!"

We saw people stop and look up, then call to us. I looked at the wadi landing strip below the village and leaned into a tight turn, taking us right over the village's main street.

Then, steering straight for the wadi, I told Ali to stay in

his sling, while I got us stopped. The yellow sand of the wadi loomed ever closer as we glided toward it. At the last moment I pulled the glider up to balance the downward force. We made a feather-soft landing.

Samson and his friend flew together in slow circles above our heads. We carried the glider back up the sloping valley to the village and were surrounded by a cheering crowd. Samson approached slowly and landed gently on Ali's shoulder. The villagers kept shouting, "Ali and Samson! Ali and Samson!"

Mustafa and his whole family danced about excitedly, asking Ali questions about what it had been like to fly. It was time for me to leave. I carried the glider to the wall, attached it to the rope, and climbed back to the top.

My remaining few weeks in Saudi Arabia went by quickly. I visited Mustafa and Ali several more times, each visit marked by changes in the village.

The last time I visited, the government had electric power working. Instead of night bringing total darkness to the village, it now had streetlights. Several rough-terrain four-wheel-drive vehicles had made it into the canyon valley, bringing government workers and equipment.

A winding road had been started from the Red Sea coast that snaked up the rugged ridges, but it was still far from completed. The all-terrain vehicles had followed the road until it ended, then made their way the remaining distance to the village. It would be years before a paved road would connect Ezratu to the rest of the world.

For the villagers, climbing up the cliff side was little help as far as contact with the outside was concerned. Once on top they faced sixty miles of desolate desert. Without camels to carry them, the trek to the nearest town was too demanding. Only the road from the west could finally bring the twentieth century to their doorstep.

We said our good-byes. I promised to keep in touch with Mustafa and his family and started toward the crevice to climb out of the canyon. The last time I saw Ali, he was waving to me from the roof of his father's house.